Three Cats Tales

Coloring Book

Shirley & Vernon Gilbert

THREE CATS TALES
COLORING BOOK

iUniverse books may be ordered through booksellers or by contacting:

iUniverse
1663 Liberty Drive
Bloomington, IN 47403
www.iuniverse.com
1-800-Authors (1-800-288-4677)

ISBN: 978-1-4917-8614-7 (sc)
ISBN: 978-1-4917-8615-4 (e)

Print information available on the last page.

iUniverse rev. date: 03/16/2016

Dedication

This Book is dedicated to the Little Ones, the Little Ones Jesus spoke for in the Bible at Matthew 18:5,6,10 and 19:14, Mark 9:42 and Luke 17:2 and elsewhere. This surely must include those Littlest Ones who never were among us, those made burnt offerings to Molech in olden times and those millions denied life by the Supreme Court in the Roe v Wade decision. The little ones, those little children allowed life by their families in our society are great blessings from our Creator and the only hope for survival for us all. They are promised a life of increased strife and diminished rewards due to our leaders' foolishness in wasting our nation's assets. These present little ones must rely on God's favor to exist in the struggle of times to come here on earth. They, like us, must rely on Jesus' loving sacrifice to attain eternal life where Satan and his minions hold no sway in affairs.

It is our hope and aim that these innocent stories can be enjoyed by little children and the adults that might read these to them. The gentle moral messages contained here reflect the gist of the Scripture given at Micah 6:8 regarding justice, mercy and humility, and in Jesus' Golden Rule. As adults read these lighthearted tales to tender ears they can remember that better times are promised by God to all of us if we will abide with the terms outlined for us at II Chronicles 7:14.

If any Little Ones are led toward the strait gate of salvation by the simple stories contained in this little book, we feel we are much more than repaid for our meager efforts.

The Authors, Shirley and Vernon Gilbert

Contents

Dedication v
Preface ix
About the Authors xi
About The Illustrator xiii

Three Cats Beginning 1
Three Cats and Brutus 2
Three Cats and The Puppy 4
Three Cats and Mean Dogs 6
Three Cats and The Cat Cartel 8
Three Cats and The Truck Ride 12
Three Cats Aiding The Law 14
Three Cats and The Toy Drone 16
Three Cats and Jealousy 19
Three Cats and The Prisoner 23
Three Cats and The Unfriendly Visitor 25
Three Cats and The Cabbie 27
Three Cats and The Billy Goat 29
Three Cats and The A.W.O.L. Canary 31
Three Cats and The Watch 33
Three Cats and The Lightning Storm 37
Three Cats and The Foul Odor 40
Three Cats and The Rendezvous 42
Three Cats and Hoppy Toad 46
Three Cats and The Fire Station Baths 48
Three Cats and The Uneaten Canary 51
Three Cats and Romo and Julie 53
Three Cats and The Raggedy Ann Doll 55
Three Cats and The Caterpillar 57
Three Cats Up The Creek Trek 59
Three Cats and The Mother Hen 62
Three Cats and The Fishing Boat 65
Three Cats Get Street Legal 68
Three Sick Cats 71
Three Cats and The Soft Spot 74
Three Cats Go Visiting 77
Three Cats Visit Two 79
Three Cats - Miss Primms 81

Three Cats and The Traffic Accident....83
Return of Alleycat....85
Three Cats Early Days....87
Three Cats and The Lineman....90
Three Cats and The Loot....92
Three Cats Visit The Mother Hen....94
Three Cats - Miss Primms - and The Board....97
Three Cats Get Inside....99
Three Cats Overnight at The Mansion....101
Three Cats and The Grand Opening....104
Three Cats and The Turtle....107
Three Cats Get Jobs....109
Three Cats - Stowaway Tomcat....111
Three Cats and The Borrowed Balloon....113
Three Cats and The Contest....115
Three Cats and The Circus....117
Three Cats and The Circus II....119
Three Cats and The Wedding....121
Three Cats Gaining Weight....123
Three Cats and Friends Go South....125
Three Cats and The Kittens....130
Three Cats and Changing Times....132
Three Cats Help Yap – Yap....134
Three Cats Returning Favors....136
Three Cats and The Squirrel....138
Three Cats Visit The Three Kittens....140
Three Cats and The Coin....142
Three Cats Plugging The Jug....144
Three Cats Tails-er-Tales Glossary....146
List of Names, Locations and Characters....148

Preface

It is our hope and desire in the writing of these stories to present Christian values to young readers. We know that these deeply held values are important to Christian parents and grandparents, so our prayer is that this book will be a reinforcement of those values that they desire to teach to their children. For instance:

The emphasizing of a mother's love and tenderness for her young, even in the animal kingdom;

The compassion and care for homeless animals which might suffer hunger and anxiety;

To do our part in helping others in time of need to make God's world a better place.

It's all here rolled into one package called "Three Cats Tales." There's mention of jealously, anger, envy, forgiveness, and the concept of the golden rule of doing unto others as you would have them do unto you. Occasionally, you will find scripture verses touched on lightly, which might spark an interest in a young child's mind to learn more about Bible teachings.

Young children all enjoy learning new "adult words" to add to their vocabulary. Some of these have been sprinkled in from time to time, complete with a glossary.

Your purchase of this book helps support Christian missionaries and the sending of books and Bibles to people around the world through the Gilbertex Foundation, Inc. May God richly bless "Three Cats Tales" and everyone who reads it.

The authors

About the Authors

Shirley and Vernon Gilbert celebrated their 62nd wedding anniversary on August 15, 2015, one day after his 83rd birthday. Without revealing Shirley's age it is proper to say she was 17, and he had just turned 21, when they were married.

They moved from Lubbock, Texas to Midland, one hundred twenty miles south, where they started an armored car service to transport money and securities between the two banks and scores of businesses. As that small start-up business grew, they branched out into other phases of security services in the small, growing West Texas oil town.

They have one daughter and three sons, who have all become involved in the business. As the business has grown, so has the family; and many of their 25 grandchildren work in the family concern. Today that business, Aprotex Corporation, provides burglar and fire alarm services to thousands of subscribers in a three state service area.

The stockholders and employees of the company all know they work for a company founded and operated on Christian principles. The Scripture of Proverbs 22:1, from the King James Bible is the company's motto; *A good name is rather to be chosen than great riches, and loving favour rather than silver and gold.*

Shirley and Vernon resigned their seats on the board at a directors meeting held at the Lubbock office on his 80th birthday, to allow more, younger directors. She still works a reduced schedule in accounting, mostly in accounts payable. He also has an office there, but spends much of his time recently in writing.

Shirley and their eldest daughter-in-law, Mona, have been kept busy lately in proofreading Vernon's writing of three previous books. The proofing sometimes results in re-writing some portions, which led to Shirley's writing some of the stories in this volume.

After three books of essays concerning the pitiful condition of our nation, resulting from secular political correctness, we enjoyed writing a collection of lighthearted banter. It is our fervent hope that our grandchildren and their generation may enjoy reading these "Three Cats Tails–er–Tales" in the freedom we enjoyed as we wrote them.

As we put the finishing touches on this work of love, such expectations appear far-fetched, but through our Savior all things are possible. He promised us at II Chronicles 7:14 this. *If my people, which are called by my name, shall humble themselves, and pray, and seek my face, and turn from their wicked ways; then will I hear from heaven, and will forgive their sin, and will heal their land ...*

The future hopes of our great grandchildren rests squarely on the shoulders of us who read these words today. Let us pray that our once great nation will abandon their worship of self, and return to the worship our forefathers exercised for the One true God of creation.

As Alleycat said when he was hoping for a nice raw steak to be discarded in the next dumpster, "IT COULD HAPPEN." Let us pray it will.

Shirley & Vernon Gilbert- August, 2015

About The Illustrator

All the sketches for this book, including the cover, are the artwork of Cameron Pryor. Cameron is not a professional artist, but was asked to do the artwork by his grandparents, the authors. Cameron is the eldest son of their daughter and son-in-law, Sherri and David Pryor. (www.Pryors.net) This couple serve as New Tribes missionaries in Chihuahua, Mexico. Cameron and his wife, Katy, serve with New Tribes in the West African nation of Senegal. They and their daughter and son, Gracia and Calvin are presently stationed there in Dakar for language studies, soon to move into the hinterlands to work with native people.

"Cameron with wife Katy, and children, Gracia and Calvin"

Cameron's sister, Autumn and her husband, Justin Bartron, and their two young sons, are with New Tribes and working in Indonesia. (www.justinandautumn.com) His remaining sister and brother are planning careers in the mission field also. Cameron is a licensed aircraft pilot and airframe and engine mechanic, qualified by the FAA to work on and repair aircraft.

Cameron and Katy are members of the Board of Directors of the Gilbertex Foundation, Inc, which is the beneficial owner of the book in your hands. All royalty income from the sale of the book accrue to the foundation, which supports missionaries and provides Bibles and Christian literature to prisons, churches, and others. To know more about the foundation, go to www.gilbertexfoundation.org.

To learn more of Cameron and Katy Pryor go to www.pryorflyer.com. To find more about New Tribes Missions go to www.ntm.org.

Every time you pick up this children's book, reflect on the work done around the world by dedicated missionaries like the Pryors and Bartrons carrying out Christ's great commission in the fields white unto harvest. You might recommend this book to your family and friends. Their kids will enjoy it, and it will help provide a Bible or help support a missionary for some poor, needy persons in a far off corner of God's beautiful planet.

The next time you see a cat, especially if you see three cats together, think of the guy, who took time to provide these illustrations, his family, and all those who serve in the front lines of spreading the Gospel of Jesus Christ.

THREE CATS BEGINNING

The year was circa 1986, the location was in San Antonio, Texas. The fifty-something granddad and grandmother had just finished a delicious supper with their son, daughter-in-law, and grandson. After enjoying a little while of visiting about family and business matters, the granddad announced the three hundred plus mile trip had left him tired and wanting to find his bed. The grandson was at the age, which has been referred to as the "terrible twos" and was being a little cranky with his mom who was clearing the table.

Thinking he would help the situation a bit, the granddad asked the tot if he would like to hear a bedtime story. In recent times they had done this to their mutual enjoyment, covering such subjects as "Little Red Riding Hood," "Hansel and Gretel," "The Three Little Pigs," and "The Three Bears" among others. When the lad feigned indifference and showed no enthusiasm, his granddad tried to sweeten the pot by asking if he wanted to hear a three pigs story or a three bears story. Little terrible two, softening a mite, jutted out his lower lip and said, "A three cats story." Granddad had never heard of such a story and neither had the lad, but they agreed on it and retired to the bedroom.

The resulting, make-it-up-as-you-go story delighted everyone, but sad to say, it is lost to anyone's recall. In ensuing years this tyke and other grandkids have heard dozens, perhaps scores of variations of the three cat's exploits. Until they grow old enough to have more adult interests, they all like the three cat's tales. In fact, some can be seen listening as old grandpa relates those unlikely episodes to their little ones.

In recent years as he has written numerous serious essays concerning horrific national and world events, he has relaxed in the world of make believe and written down a few of those innocent ramblings of the mind, recounting the outrageous antics of the three cats. These can probably be counted among the dreams of old men mentioned in the Bible at Joel 2:28 and Acts 2:7. If they should inspire the younger generations to see the visions mentioned there, it could be a good thing.

It is hoped these unlikely stories may entertain and inspire the reader. When you have suffered through these poor efforts, check out the ones by Aesop. The old granddad responsible for these, read many of "Aesop's Fables" about three score and ten years ago. Any resemblance between the two should be chalked up to coincidence, not plagiarism.... Happy reading.

THREE CATS AND BRUTUS

There have been some questions and misinformation regarding the three cats. This memo is offered to help clear up those matters.

The three cats are identified by the names: Yellowcat, Alleycat, and Tomcat. Yellowcat is a, well ..., yellow colored feline with a hint of tiger stripes in his fur. Alleycat is a somewhat unkempt looking fellow that is kind of muckley-dunn colored, with hints of catsup, mustard, and whatever else might be in the dumpster, where he gets most of his food. He loves to spin yarns about feeding the whole family with his catching of mice, rats and cottontail rabbits. (He has been seen actually catching butterflies and grasshoppers.) Tomcat is a black and white cat that looks a little like a miniature Holstein dairy cow.

The three cats live, mostly, in a cardboard box behind the dumpster in the alley between Elm and Cherry Avenues, just off Main Street in Centerville, which is a seacoast town. They go to Fire Station #3, where all the firefighters like them and treat them really well. Sometimes the cleanup crew put some tasty scraps left from a station meal aside for them. Upon occasion, they stop by the police station and fancy themselves as police cats that can do things the dumb police dogs can't accomplish. The police are a great bunch, who take very seriously their commitment to help one another, including the meter maids and animal control officers. However, they pride themselves in serving the public also. Once, when the three cats were there in the squad room basking by the potbellied stove, and the animal control officer pulled into the parking lot, Sergeant O'Malley quickly opened the door to the locker room and shooed the trio inside. When a couple of the other officers teased him about harboring fugitives, he retorted that the man is known as a *dog*catcher with stress on dog.

When the weather is nice, the trio sometimes venture all the way to the docks, where the fishermen bring their catch to be processed. They help themselves to any stray fish that might accidentally drop onto the loading dock. Some of the crews aren't too nice to the cats and try to shoo them away, but others treat them like pets and feed them choice morsels and even, sometimes, invite them on-board the fishing boat. Tomcat and Yellowcat really like that, but Alleycat says the boat makes him seasick.

Not too far from the fire station is Otto's Meat Market owned by ..., who else, Mr. Otto. When he is in a good mood he has been known to give the cats scraps of tasty meat, even the heel end of a German sausage. Once Tomcat slipped inside the back door, and Mr. Otto helped him back outside with a pretty big broom. The next couple of times they went foraging to the meat market there were only two cats who went. Tomcat told them, "Just bring me back something."

Mrs. Pennyrich, the wealthy widow, who lives in the big house that covers a whole block on Sterling Avenue has a big mean-looking bulldog named Brutus, that every dog and cat and most humans are wary of. Brutus likes the three cats and gladly shares his fancy food with them. This is because they once found Mrs. Pennyrich's rare imported kitten, Fluffy, and returned him to Brutus, who had gone to sleep and let him escape from his care in the big backyard. The missus doesn't understand why Brutus allows those mangy stray cats into the yard, and he wouldn't want to explain it to her even if he could talk.

It is hoped this brief memo will serve to clear up a few questions that some have expressed pertaining to the three cats. With this information as a guide, everyone can better understand future news releases pertaining to this famous (in the alley between Elm and Cherry, near Main, at least) trio, the three cats.

THREE CATS AND THE PUPPY

It is an established scientific fact that members of the feline group (that's cats) can communicate with one another. They can communicate to a limited extent with other animal species also. When they're happy they purr, and when they want something they meow, and when they're unhappy they hiss, or growl, or roar, or claw, owing to just how unhappy they are. That roar is reserved for the king of the cats, the African lion. In talking to dogs, they mostly use hissing, growling and clawing, especially clawing. When, on rare occasion, a cat is seen cuddling and purring with a member of the canine family (that's dogs) it is notable enough to make the six o'clock news. Mother dogs have been known to take care of kittens, and mother cats have sometimes tenderly tended to little puppies. Not very often, and these events make the national news.

Once upon a time the three cats, Yellowcat, Tomcat, and Alleycat, were enjoying a quiet evening at home in their cardboard box/home behind the alley dumpster. They had just finished sharing a meal from stuff that Alleycat retrieved from the dumpster behind Otto's Meat Market and were recounting each one's deeds for the day. They heard a vehicle enter the alley from Cherry Street. Cats have good ears, and they knew right away that this vehicle wasn't Officer O'Malley's squad car, or the trash truck or the meter reader's pickup. As it came closer, they all three froze in terror as they recognized the city dogcatcher's pickup. You see, he's called the dogcatcher, but he also catches stray cats and other homeless animals, which he takes to the pound, where they are confined in cages. Cats don't like cages.

As they heard the dogcatcher continue down the alley, not even slowing as he passed their box behind the dumpster, they all gave a sigh of relief. Then they heard a rustling among the papers and trash beside their dumpster. Along with their hearing the rustling, they also got a whiff of dog smell. Cats have very good noses. Yellowcat peered into the darkness (cats have very, very good eyes with superior night vision) and there was a little puppy shaking with fear, while hiding among the trash on the ground. Tomcat whispered, "Is it a dog?" Yellowcat replied that it was a dog, a little dog, a puppy. The little dog was naturally afraid of cats, but the man with the net on a pole had chased and tried to catch him and this ole yellow cat was purring. Dogs don't purr, but they all know that purring is a good sign in a cat. Whimpering a little, the puppy allowed Yellowcat to help him inside the three cats' home.

The three cats made their new visitor welcome; Alleycat even licked him a little. Dogs and cats and many other animals lick one another to show kindness and care. They sometimes even do this with humans. If a kitten licks you it's okay. If a grizzly bear licks you, it's time to be somewhere else - fast. After making the baby dog feel at home, the whole crew snuggled up and went fast asleep with happy dreams. The puppy had found helpful friends in time of need, and the three cats had been able to extend a helping hand to a needy fellow critter.

Early next morning, they were all awakened by the sound of a vehicle entering slowly from Elm Avenue. Their first thought was that it might be the city dogcatcher returning. As the car slowly came closer, the three cats relaxed as they could tell by the sound that it wasn't the dogcatcher. Then they heard a lady's voice calling, "Titan - Titan, where are you?" With this the little dog jumped up so high he bumped the top of the cardboard box and let out a loud "Erf-erf-erf," as he was too young to say arf. The big car stopped and a freckled-faced boy jumped out and scooped up the puppy who had bounded from the three cats' box home into the alley. The boy was laughing and holding the little dog up for the lady in the car to see.

"Titan!" exclaimed Tomcat, "What a big strong name for such a little whiny dog," and they all three laughed as the family drove off. Have you never heard a cat laugh? Well they can, but like their talk to one another, only cats can hear and understand it. Cats can communicate with us like the ways mentioned earlier and by bristling up their hair when upset. When a special kind of cat, a skunk, turns around and raises his tail it is a special warning. We can discuss the three cats' half cousin, Pepe Phew, next time perhaps.

THREE CATS AND MEAN DOGS

The three cats were having a grocery delivery problem. You see, there is a big group of stray dogs in the neighborhood that are smarter than the city animal control officer. (That's what the mayor calls the dogcatcher when he is turning down a raise for him.) These mean natured dogs are really bad when it comes to dealing with cats, especially cats that don't have license tags and a home with a fence to protect them. This pack of stray dogs noticed Yellowcat returning from a successful foraging trip that included a very good stop at Mr. Otto's Meat Market. The dogs forced Yellowcat to turn around at the entrance to his alley and run out of their sight. Being lazy, they just returned to the alley entrance to wait, until Yellowcat returned to try again to get to his home he shared with Alleycat and Tomcat.

Being smarter than both the dogcatcher and the dogs, Yellowcat went around the block to enter the alley where there were no dogs. The three cats were discussing this problem and eating their good scraps from Otto's, when a delivery truck slowly drove up the alley and a black "cat" with white stripes dropped himself down from his hiding/riding place under the truck, onto the alley's gravel surface. Thus arrived the three cat's half cousin, Pepe Phew. Pepe had hitchhiked in from his home in the country, just to visit his city half cousins. The three cats were, as always, very happy to see their brash family member since his visits were so much fun. They shared their food with him and the story of the troubles Yellowcat had encountered running the dog blockade.

Meanwhile, those smart/dumb dogs figured out how Yellowcat outsmarted them and got his groceries delivered. They decided to split up and guard both entrances to the alley whenever they saw any of the three cats going dumpster diving for food. (Cats can easily climb upon and get down into most dumpsters, but most dogs can't.)

This new policy of the dogs concerned the three cats and they were afraid they would not be able to bring food home anymore. Dogs fight among themselves over any scrap of food, but cats enjoy sharing among family and buddies. (Some exceptions apply.)

Pepe, being a skunk, isn't too much worried about a few dogs with bad table manners. Like all skunks, Pepe has a powerful defensive weapon. When disturbed, a skunk can point his rear end at a foe and squirt a stream of very foul-smelling stuff that makes the biggest, baddest dog whimper and cry like a little puppy.

With their plans made, the four cats left home to go looking for food. Of course, the sentry dogs stirred from their lazy naps and wondered among themselves about the new cat with the bushy tail and police car paint job. When the four cats returned with their collection of goodies, the guarding dogs quit wondering because they found out about the fourth cat.

When the bully dogs growled their warnings, the cats turned around and the dogs thought a fun chase was about to begin. Instead, the cats stood their ground and all four raised their tails aimed directly at the dumb dogs. Those dumb dogs never knew who or how many cats did it to them, because Pepe, being experienced in the matter, covered all of the dogs with a fine, stinking spray that rendered the dogs blind for a while and made all of them sick to their stomachs.

The word got around among the worthless dog community about this event, and the four cats were able to do their grocery shopping and visiting. Cats love to visit friends and purr together without any interference by any of the dumb dogs. When Pepe left to go home by sneaking up under a UPS truck headed for the country delivery route, the dogs weren't sure he didn't leave his secret chemical weapon with his city half cousins. From that day on, when confronted by dogs, the three cats always turn around, and if they raise their tail, the dogs are somewhere else ASAP.

THREE CATS AND THE CAT CARTEL

Some cats will go out of their way to get into a good catfight. That is, fights between cats, without any dogs, lawn mowers, or guns involved. Even little kittens, brothers and sisters, enjoy play fighting with one another, not using their little claws and teeth to really hurt. Some grown tomcats are very mean to other, usually smaller, weaker cats. That's one reason every housewife with cats needs a good sturdy broom. Homeless cats, with no broom-wielding referee, must use their brains to think of ways to stay clear of problems with other cats, and other different troubles that come up.

The three cats, Yellowcat, Tomcat, and Alleycat, began last fall to have troubles brought upon them in the form of some mean, old cats that took over the neighborhood. This gang of bad cats were too lazy and trifling to find food for themselves, so they just took whatever others had for their own enjoyment.

Cats don't have hands, so they have to carry in their mouths, whatever they want to move somewhere. Have you ever seen a mama cat taking her little kittens somewhere? She picks the little ones up by the nape of their neck with her mouth and can actually run and jump if necessary while not hurting her baby, as it allows her to transport it. A mama cat is sort of like us humans. She can kill a bird for supper with her powerful jaws and sharp teeth. Likewise, we can use our mouths to help and comfort others, or we can use them to hurt and gossip about others. Just as the mama cat would never harm her kittens, we should be very careful that we don't harm our family, or friends, or neighbors with careless words or actions.

Yellowcat was returning home, (home being the cardboard box behind the dumpster in the alley) with a mouthful of goodies he had found discarded by some people who were barbequing in their backyard. Well, actually one big, fat wiener hadn't really been discarded, but it did drop onto the lawn when he rubbed himself against the leg of the little table by the grill. I mean, it did fall on the ground, and he just got it and ran under the fence into the alley with it. The cook tried to get it before it hit the grass, but missed. Yellowcat didn't miss (cats are very quick), and when the cook yelled "SCAT!" it scared Yellowcat and he fled, but he didn't drop that nice, fat wiener. As I started to say – he was headed home with his goodies when he saw the scroungy lookout cat for the cat cartel lounging under a bush at the mouth of his alley.

Yellowcat didn't miss a beat. He just made a u-turn and went around the block to enter the other end of his alley. That old lazy lookout cat never even stirred. When Yellowcat got closer to the other end of his alley, he was upset to find the cartel had another lookout posted there too. Before that old lazy crook stirred, Yellowcat did another uey and carried his load of goodies to the middle of the block, looking for some alternate route home. Meanwhile, that nice, fat, warm wiener was making him struggle to not stop and have an early supper by himself. Then he saw that the Martin family's sedan was not parked in their driveway. This was good news, because the Martins always took their yapping dog with them whenever they went shopping. Yellowcat can easily out run that yap-yap dog, but maybe not, with a mouthful of goodies.

Yellowcat went quickly underneath the gate into the Martin's backyard and across the patio to the back fence. There, he dropped his mouthful of good stuff and meowed for his buddies to come help him. When he assured Tomcat and Alleycat that old yap-yap was gone, they scurried up the wooden gate and jumped down inside the yard. Cats love to scurry, climb obstacles, and jump long distances to land as light as a feather. It's a cat thing.

Yellowcat was so happy to see his pals and have their help that he only let out a very muted growl when one of them started to take that fat wiener. This was his way of saying "I'll bring this, and you can help with some of the other loot ..., er food."

With the food safely inside their home, the three cats enjoyed their shared meal and purred contentedly awhile before taking a nice restful catnap. Meanwhile, the cartel cats, including the shiftless lookouts, were having stomach grumbles from getting hungrier and hungrier.

The next morning, the three cats got going early, before the worthless cartel crooks even stirred. On their way to find breakfast, they went down to the truck depot where they have a friend who rides with an assistant (I almost said his owner, but dogs have owners, cats have staff and helpers.) to make out-of-town deliveries. They asked him to get a message to their half cousin, Bobbycat, who lives in a nearby town. The message was delivered, and as requested, Bobbycat arrived at their house (cardboard box) late one afternoon. They had maneuvered a really big box that had originally held a television set, into place next to their box and put some nice paper and soft rags in there to make Bobby comfortable. Cats, even big cats like soft comfortable places to relax. Speaking of big! Bobbycat's mother is a fluffy tabby cat, and his daddy is a real, sure-'nuff bobcat. Bobby isn't as big as his dad, but he's lots bigger than his mother, or any of the regular felines around town. He's about as much muscle and bone as all three of his half cousins put together.

After breakfast, the three cats started up the alley, and the cartel cats noted that they turned, as if to go to Otto's Meat Market. The boss (boss because he's biggest and meanest) outlaw cat said, "Looks like we're gonna have German sausage for lunch, heh-heh." Soon, the three cats returned, each one with nice amounts of scraps from Otto's. When the cartel lookout alerted his comrades-in-crime, they came running to get their share. That's when Alleycat dropped his load, and let out a blood-curdling yowl. This was a prearranged signal for Bobbycat to introduce himself to the cartel crowd. He came quick as lightning, and roaring like thunder. When the crooks saw his size and his speed, they scattered like scraps of paper in a whirlwind.

The three cats, with their oversized cousin, laughed all the way to lunch in Bobbycat's big house. The next time they were returning with some fish from Fulton Street Fish Market, the cartel bunch let them pass unhindered, but started following them in a threatening manner as they went down the alley toward home. On a quiet signal from Tomcat, cousin Bobbycat charged out of his big box and leaping completely over his family cats, landed in the midst of the outlaw cats, and none too softly either. He managed to bump into every one of them as they scattered like cockroaches in a flashlight beam. When he was finished thumping the bad guys, he extended his large, sharp claws and ripped long slashes into their guard post plywood. It looked like Zorro's signature, only bigger and deeper. The gas company (which owns the plywood sign) left it there, but it's hard to read the gas main warning printed on it, because of the long, deep scratches up higher than many dog's backs.

After this, the cartel kind of moved their headquarters further west, and some even started finding their own groceries in honorable (by feline standards that is) ways, like stealing dog's food and catching mice and rats. Whenever one of them ventured to make a quick run through the three cats' alley, he would see that big box still there and didn't slow down to try to find out if that monster cat was still there too.

The three cats enjoyed Bobbycat's visit, and he repaid their food sharing by bringing in fare for the table. (Well, cats don't usually eat at a table, but it sounds nicer than saying, "Fare for the floor," don't you think?) Bobby could catch a rabbit as easily as they could catch a grasshopper. When time came for Bobbycat to return home, he told them to just let him know if they had any more trouble he could help with. He promised that he would visit in the future whenever he got a chance. He said he would rather not visit when their other half cousin, Pepe Phew was there. Once in years past at a family get-together, he and Pepe got into a heated argument about politics, and when Bobby made the mistake of growling at Pepe, and Pepe ..., well, that's another tale for another time.

THREE CATS AND THE TRUCK RIDE

By now we all know who the three cats are: Yellowcat, Alleycat, and Tomcat. This story is mostly about Yellowcat and a mess he got himself into once a few years ago. It all started because of the trait common to all cats, the fact that they are inquisitive. That means they are nosy and always checking everything out. They always want to learn new things for themselves, but you can't teach them very easily.

Yellowcat had been hunting grasshoppers and field mice in the big, vacant lot between the church and the creek. He was lazily returning home with a full stomach when he saw the UPS truck parked at the back door to the church. He wandered that direction to see what was going on. He saw the driver roll his dolly up the ramp at the truck's rear roll-up door and go inside the building with some papers. As he got closer, Yellowcat detected a smell of cooked food coming from the truck. As we have discussed before, cats have very sensitive noses. Now Yellowcat's stomach was full, and he wasn't hungry in the least, but cats always go out of their way to check out good smells.

Yellowcat glanced around to see that the coast was clear and quickly scampered up the ramp into the truck. That smell was coming from somewhere up front, somewhere past the high stack of boxes and cartons. Yellowcat, without stopping to think, began hopping atop the boxes and moving closer to the front and away from the open tailgate. We've discussed before that almost all cats are pretty good at scampering, jumping, and climbing. Just as Yellowcat got to the front of the stacks of boxes, he knew that good smell was coming from somewhere near the floor. Then, he heard the ramp sliding back into place and the big door closing!

Soon the engine started and the truck was in motion. Those cardboard boxes were slick and the truck was lurching quite a bit. Cats don't like motion and traveling. Slipping and sliding on the boxes made Yellowcat very apprehensive. That means uneasy or scared, so he hunkered down. If you don't know what that means, just think of a car with no wheels. When the truck stopped, Yellowcat jumped down to the floor, where there was some wood surface that he could get his claws into, to help him keep his balance. There it was on the floor right in front of him, the small half of a hamburger in the wrapper. Yellowcat was still full and was a little queasy from the motion; he had lost his interest in food.

The delivery driver opened the big door and unloaded some boxes, but Yellowcat stayed out of sight because he felt as if the man would not be happy if he found him in his truck. This happened several times, and Yellowcat stayed hidden behind the dwindling stacks of boxes, as he could tell they were farther and farther from downtown. Cats can tell when they are getting close to home somehow.

Once at a stop, the driver reloaded several boxes in a front corner of the truck, close to where Yellowcat was hiding. When the door was closed, he got himself in the corner behind those boxes. Soon, the truck made a rather long drive in highway traffic, into downtown traffic and then parked. Then, the driver shut down the engine and left the truck. There was Yellowcat, alone and unable to leave the closed truck. He found a place with some soft paper on the floor and happy for the stopped motion, curled up for a long catnap. Cats all like soft places and naps.

Next morning, before things were stirring at the UPS yard, Yellowcat woke up and remembered that piece of a burger. He wanted some liquid to lap up, but made do without as he ate the meat patty first and then the bun, where there wasn't too much mustard. He left the lettuce for someone else, who might be hungrier than he was.

The driver and some others loaded lots and lots of new boxes and cartons. Yellowcat stayed behind the returned boxes in the front corner. Soon the engine started and the truck began to move. Yellowcat stayed hunkered down on the floor. At each stop he would climb to a top box where he could see out the big door. Soon he saw a scene he was familiar with, near to his alley. He scampered to the rear boxes and took a flying leap to the ramp and street. The driver said, "I thought I saw a little tiger flying like a bird ..., too much coffee, I guess." Welcome home Yellowcat!

THREE CATS AIDING THE LAW

The three cats, Tomcat, Yellowcat, and Alleycat, had been busy all day chasing butterflies, hunting mice, and dumpster diving. They were exhausted and full of discarded pizza. They had been sleeping peacefully in their big cardboard box/home behind the dumpster in the Cherry Street alley, when noises of a commotion awakened them. First they heard tires squealing and engines revving and then men yelling. They also heard racing footsteps in the alley. They heard the police radios and the police themselves calling to one another. Then they heard someone running towards them and stopping. That person raised the squeaking lid of the dumpster, jumped in, and closed the lid.

Alleycat, who had been sleeping closest to the opening of their home, carefully looked out and pulled his head back inside. He told Yellowcat and Tomcat that there were police cars at both ends of the alley and another car stopped in the alley just short of Cherry Street with people everywhere. Tomcat looked out and saw the policemen take two perps (that's short for perpetrators) into the paddy wagon. Back to that word, it means someone who commits an act, or does something. Sometimes the police officers refer to such people as suspects or actors, but the three cats overheard the younger detectives at the precinct station saying "perps" and thought it sounded cool, so they liked to use it, too.

Now, back to what was happening in the alley. After the paddy wagon left and while the wrecker was hooking up to the bad guys' car, the sergeant was telling his crew that there were two robbers in the store and a third one driving the getaway car. So, they were looking everywhere for the missing robber. One of the officers overturned the three cat's box and exclaimed, "There's a nest of cats here!" Another turned his flashlight on them and told the first one to not bother them and fix their box back into place. He told him they were Sergeant O' Malley's pets, that he always fed whenever they showed up at the station on day shift.

About that time, a muffled sneeze came from the dumpster, and the policemen became very quiet as the one nearest to the dumpster flipped the lid and ordered the perp inside to come out with his hands up. After they frisked and cuffed him, they loaded him into one of the squad cars and transported him. Transported is cop talk for taking him to the station house. Soon it became quiet in the alley, and the crickets resumed their serenade, or else it was a mockingbird mimicking the crickets. Who can tell? Even cats with their keen ears are hard pressed to tell for sure. Once Yellowcat and Alleycat were discussing this, and Alleycat said he had a surefire way to tell which it was. Yellowcat retorted, "Yeah, and just how do you do that?" Alleycat grinned and replied, "If it has a wingspan of over a foot and makes a whole meal, it sure ain't no cricket."

After things got quiet, the three cats went back to sleep, only to be reawakened by a patrol car coming into the alley and two officers looking around among the weeds and trash. They were talking about a handheld radio that was missing. One would move apart from his partner and softly count into his radio, while the other one listened for the lost radio's sound. They did this for some time before moving on elsewhere. The three cats could hear them when they were quite far away. As we have mentioned before, cats have very good ears. Soon it became evident that what they were hearing wasn't the officers themselves, because they heard the patrol car leave. They got out of their box/home and soon discovered the missing handheld radio under an old, discarded mattress. The three cats tried to see if they might be able to return the radio to the station house, but it was too heavy and bulky and had a long, coiled cable connecting the speaker/mic. to the unit. What to do ..., but Tomcat hit on an idea. With his paws he held the button down on the microphone and meowed into it.

At headquarters the dispatcher in the radio room was perplexed, thinking some officer was cutting up, so he scolded the unofficial use of the radio. Tomcat sent another signal, and soon an appreciative Sergeant O' Malley, who had just come on duty, drove up with a hearty laugh and a bag of donuts for the three cats. He was very proud of them ... and they were, too.

THREE CATS AND THE TOY DRONE

The three cats – Tomcat, Yellowcat, and Alleycat, were enjoying a nice, quiet catnap in their big cardboard box/home on a warm, summer afternoon. The sun had just gone behind the dumpster, so the temperature was easing somewhat, and life was good. Suddenly there was a whirring sound which made the snoozing cats' ears perk up in their sleep. Then there was a crashing sound, and something bumped loudly against their box, making it shake a lot. All three cats were instantly awake and excited. Yellowcat said "Whatwuzthat?" Neither of the others answered because nobody knew what it was that woke them up. Cats can talk to one another and understand what sounds to you and me as just meowing, hissing, growling, and snarling.

If you are coloring would you like to close the box, leaving a corner flap opening?

Tomcat ventured to the flap door of the box and looked outside, but he couldn't see what had caused all the racket and made the box shake so badly. With the others' encouragement, he cautiously crept around the edge of the box and quickly returned. Tomcat said there was a big kite crashed between their box and the tall fence bordering the alley. Not only that, but there was a shiny black machine of some kind tangled up in the kite's tail. Alleycat asked if that shiny black thing might be a crow, since he's always thinking of something to eat. Tomcat replied that it was a machine of some sort, not a bird. The cats were familiar with kites since a few had landed in their alley in the past, and the owners followed the string to find where their kites had come to earth. Checking this kite showed there was no long kite string attached, only a few feet. No noisy boys came looking for it either. Soon it came nightfall, and the three cats checked out the nearby dumpsters for their supper and curled up for a good night's sleep.

Next morning they were hardly awake before they heard a vehicle coming slowly up the alley. They knew it wasn't the garbage truck, a police cruiser, nor the dogcatcher. They knew by heart those particular engine sounds, so they peeked out and saw a long, blue limo driven by a man wearing a chauffeur's cap. In the passenger seats were a young woman and a small boy. The limo stopped, and the driver got out and inspected the inside of the dumpster. He returned to the big car and told the boy, "No luck, Percy." The boy held up a black box with an antenna on it and told the chauffeur the transponder from his drone was sending a strong signal when he pressed the locate button on his control console. The man slowly shook his head and got back into the limo and proceeded slowly up the alley and turned to the right on Cherry Street.

The three cats discussed these strange happenings, and decided the people in the big, blue car were looking for the contraption tangled in the kite's tail hidden out of sight behind their cardboard box/home. Midmorning, after a good trip to the garbage can behind Otto's Meat Market, the three cats were enjoying breakfast at home. They heard the now familiar sound of the powerful engine of the big, blue limo as it entered their alley from Cherry Street. Yellowcat was nearest the flap door, and he ran into the center of the alley just in front of the slowly moving car and stopped. The driver also stopped the big car, and Yellowcat promptly jumped upon the hood, where his claws slipped on the waxed surface, making him slide clear to the windshield. The three people inside all laughed at this, and the driver got out to see if Yellowcat was all right. With this, Tomcat and Alleycat came out to see what was happening. The small boy left his control box in the car and came to where all three cats were with the man. Alleycat tugged at the boy's pants leg and walked to where the boy could see the kite with his drone. The boy was very happy to see his drone and picked it and Alleycat up and ran joyfully to the mistress. She said "Percy, put that filthy animal down, there's no telling what it might have!" When the excitement died down, she felt badly for her outburst and instructed the chauffeur to bring the three cats some food as a reward for their help. When he did so later that day, he had a big box of cat food in plastic packages. He set it down behind their box/home and told them he had brought this particular kind since he knew cats don't have can openers, but are all equipped by nature with plastic bag openers.

For the next few weeks, they were all glad that toy drone was not a crow.

You might like to re-draw the Cats' box here with the flap door.

THREE CATS AND JEALOUSY

The three cats we are familiar with, Tomcat, Yellowcat, and Alleycat, have been close pals for a long time and are usually seen together in whatever thing they are doing. Sometimes they go their separate ways for a while, but almost always they are back together by nightfall. They are interested in what the others are doing and enjoy seeing their comrades'* successes and good fortune. When one of them enjoys good times, they all join in celebrating it.

One afternoon Tomcat was returning home from hunting for food, when he was passing behind a large mansion in the alley. The wealthy lady who lived there was in the garden with the gardener, examining some flowers he had recently planted. Tomcat stopped and was watching what they were doing, hoping they might be bringing some table scrap, type garbage to the dumpster in the alley. No such luck. He was starting to resume his homeward trek* when the lady exclaimed, "Look Moses, there's a nice looking cat marked just like our Bobo was." She came through the iron gate into the alley and started sweet talking to Tomcat, while also sending Moses to get some food to entice Tomcat into coming to her. Cats understand people pretty well, not the exact words so much as the tone of their voices and their body language as they talk to the cat.

The smallish Moses scurried into the big house and quickly returned with some sliced ham and cold gravy from the kitchen. The nice lady set the food down just inside the gate and offered it to Tomcat with soft words and slow movements designed to instill confidence in him. Tomcat could smell the ham and that aroma meant as much to him as the encouraging sounding words from the lady.

He slowly moved towards the food, while keeping a wary eye on Moses. Cats trust ladies and kids more readily than they do men and big boys. Was that ham good! And the gravy tasted much better than it looked to be. Of course, when it was all gone except a little ham he wanted to take home to share with his buddies, he sat down and commenced licking and cleaning his paws and whiskers as all cats do. The lady exclaimed, "Moses, he acts just like our Bobo did when he enjoyed food – I think he is telling us thanks." With that, Tomcat took the remaining ham and quickly slipped under the iron gate into the alley and toward home and his pals.

Alleycat and Yellowcat were very interested in the nice ham, but less interested in where Tomcat acquired* it. He didn't even mention the name "Bobo" the nice lady tagged him with. Two days later Tomcat took the same route returning home and lingered a little near the iron alley gate. The gardener spied him and dropped his spade and hurried inside. Soon the lady came out with him and was carrying some fancy cat food while sweet talking to her "Bobo" and inviting him into the backyard garden. Remembering the tasty ham, Tomcat/Bobo shot under the gate and commenced to purr loudly and gobble up the savory* cat food. The lady exclaimed, "Look Moses, he purrs and eats too fast just like Bobo did. This seems to prove reincarnation just like the Yoga* meditation guru* teaches." Not understanding all that gibberish, Tomcat took the last unopened packet of fancy grub and hurriedly scooted under the gate and headed home.

The next time Tomcat ventured to the iron alley gate, he had his two friends with him. They were hoping to scarf up some of those blue ribbon victuals* themselves, since the paltry portions Tomcat was able to bring home had whetted* their appetites. Again, Moses was in the garden wrestling with some stubborn water hose. He called the lady of the house to let her know Bobo was in the alley again. She appeared on the back porch, calling for Bobo to come into the garden with sweet words of encouragement. Then she saw his two friends and shrieked, "Don't allow those two horrid alley cats inside the property." Cats can easily tell when they aren't wanted, so those two horrid alley cats left in a hurry. The lady came closer and soothingly called her Bobo to come inside to enjoy some chicken she had prepared in anticipation of his visit. Tomcat/Bobo felt a little embarrassed at her treatment of his pals, but he overcame that, when he smelled the aroma from the chicken supper she was offering. When he finally got home his friends greeted him with derisive calls of "What leftover scraps did 'Bobo baby' bring us from his fancy big home and his big mama?"

Tomcat retorted, "I didn't bring you anything, since you didn't stay for supper." This, of course set the mood for a somewhat icy evening, rather than the usual friendly period they normally enjoyed before sleepy time. Tomcat continued to be Bobo and enjoy the special treatment at the big house. At the lady's invitation he began to take catnaps in a fluffy basket she placed near the backdoor. She even had Moses install a pet door there so Bobo could come and go at his good pleasure.

The first time Bobo stayed overnight at the big house, the other two cats worried about his safety and didn't sleep too soundly. Early the next morning they went to the iron gate and watched. Sure enough, soon after Moses came from the tool shed with rake and shovel, Tomcat came out through the pet door and strolled behind the gardener. Yellowcat and Alleycat were relieved to see Tomcat safe and well, but pretty jealous of him at the same time. There he was – living like the king of the jungle, while they were worrying about him! Their jealousy turned into envy, and their envy into anger.

Bobo really enjoyed his special status in his newly adopted home – the coolness on hot days and the adoration his new mistress had for him and her approval of anything he did. He began to think pretty highly of himself, and to think he could do no wrong. His old pals meanwhile, thought not-too-kind thoughts about him and disdainfully* began to refer to him as "Boob-o", as they made catty remarks about him and his lofty lifestyle.

At times, when he was alone with his thoughts, Tomcat reminisced* about his past, living in the old cardboard box behind the dumpster in the alley with his best buddies. They were always there to help one another. In those reflective periods, Tomcat sometimes wished he had never heard of Bobo. He wondered how his pals were doing – if they were well and happy – if they were missing him like he was missing them. He noticed he was getting fat, so fat in fact the pet door was getting kinda tight. He really wished he had been kinder to them the day the lady shooed them away. He wished he had gone with them. He wondered if they would welcome him back home.

At times, when they were talking to one another, Yellowcat and Alleycat thought of old times, when Tomcat was with them and they had enjoyed the good comradery* of depending on one another.

They missed his loyalty and reliability. They admitted to one another that they were both ashamed of being jealous of his good fortune and envying his circumstances. They both wished Tom would leave Bobo where he found him and come back home with them.

Tomcat left his breakfast of shrimp soufflé* half eaten and hurried to Otto's Meat Market's dumpster. He was thinking of the tasty sausage scraps sometimes to be found there; mostly he was thinking he might happen to meet his old home buddies there. No such luck – then as he was leaving, he met them in the entrance from Main Street. Forgotten were the hard feelings, envy and jealousy. Remembered were the good times of the past as they scurried, as a team, to see what gems of goodness Otto might have left for them.

Tomcat knew the nice lady at the big house would miss him, and he felt bad about that. As the three cats returned to their box/home they were planning a return visit with her as a trio of friends. They all three agreed they hoped the lady would accept Bobo – er Tomcat's horrid friends for a short visit.

*Meaning of some words used. If you already know them, good for you.

Acquired – gotten, received.
Comrades – close friends in united effort.
Trek – a long or difficult trip or journey.
Savory – tasty, flavorful.
Whetted – sharpened, enhanced.
Yoga – special physical exercises bordering on a religion.
Guru – a trusted teacher of higher learning.
Disdainfully – showing no concern for others.
Reminisced – recalled, remembered with fondness.

Comradery – mutual trust and close friendship among comrades. (Also, camaraderie in some uses.)
Soufflé – fancy food made fluffy with whipped egg whites.
Victuals – food.

You can draw the big iron gate here like you think it looks.

THREE CATS AND THE PRISONER

The three cats – Alleycat, Tomcat, and Yellowcat, have several good places to "shop" for food. The prices are right, because they never have to pay anything for what they eat. There are a few backyards in their neighborhood where homeowners feed their own pets, which our three cats can access easily. One such location has a very high, concrete block fence to keep out intruders, but a large, old oak tree grows just outside the fence. With its strong branches growing out over the backyard, and cats' fondness for climbing trees, and the lush, soft grass to alight upon ... well you get the picture. Trees figure into the three cats' menu planning from time to time, given the fact that birds are an important part of free cats' food regimen. Cats kept indoors can't enjoy this food item unless perhaps someone accidentally lets the canary or parrot escape, heh heh. In addition to the backyard pet buffet, there is also the backyard barbecue scene, where a fast moving cat with good timing, can score a hamburger patty, or a hot dog wiener or sausage.

In addition to the backyard opportunities, there are numerous places that offer the thinking feline a chance to fill his stomach with prime victuals. The wharf where the fishing boats unload their catch and where an occasional stray fish may fall from an overloaded basket or conveyor belt, is a good bet. Then there are the several restaurants and cafes where careless workers leave the dumpster or garbage container unclosed sometimes. The competition at some of these venues can be fierce, since many other cats fail to be as nice and considerate as our three cats. Once Tomcat suffered a black eye from a scuffle with a larger, not-so-nice ruffian cat behind the Red Lobster. He may have suffered two black eyes, but you couldn't tell since one of his eyes is normally surrounded with black hair anyway.

The one best place for good stuff for our three cats is Otto's Meat Market, since Mr. Otto shoos all other cats from behind his place except the chosen three, whom he favors.

One afternoon the trio were at the large dumpster behind Otto's and the lid was open. It was not opened fully with the lid thrown back in horizontal position, but standing about vertical. No problem, plenty of room to get inside to discover whatever tasty morsels were to be found, so Alleycat jumped to the lip of the top and jumped again down inside. About the time he hit bottom, a stray gust of wind caused the heavy metal lid to fall closed with a loud bang. What to do? Tomcat and Yellowcat were powerless to move the cover and Alleycat inside, wasn't even able to get up to it from his position inside. The duo outside felt hopeless and worried that Alleycat might feel abandoned. They decided to wait and see if Mr. Otto or one of the helpers would maybe come out to discard some stuff, so Alleycat could escape from his prison. Soon, one of the young workers came out the back door and their spirits soared. The man only straightened some crates and retrieved a mop and broom and returned inside.

Soon the lights inside the market were turned out, and Mr. Otto and the others came out the front door and all said good night and departed in their cars and on their bicycles. It became very quiet so the two, free cats went to the dumpster to try to communicate with their trapped pal. They found it to be impossible due to the heavy, thick metal walls. They even tried scratching the big box's walls, but the surface was so slick there was no way to make any sound that way.

Tomcat and Yellowcat decided they would stay there for the night to be able to welcome Alleycat, when the dumpster was first opened in the morning. They knew they would want him to do that for them if they were the ones inside. A little before midnight some kids driving by on the street threw some trash out of their car as they sped by the alley. Tomcat and Yellowcat went to check it out. They found the big half of a hamburger and a good amount of french fries, still warm. With plenty of good water from the dripping tap next door, they enjoyed a nice meal. The burger was with mayo, not mustard and hold the onions too. Most cats don't prefer mustard or onions. With almost full tummies, they worried that Alleycat could be hungry because sometimes they found only butcher paper and sawdust swept from the shop's floor in this dumpster. They only slept fitfully as they thought of their pal's plight. Next morning when a worker opened the lid, Alleycat somewhat slowly climbed out and they anxiously asked if he was okay. An overstuffed Alleycat replied "**BURRP.**"

THREE CATS AND THE UNFRIENDLY VISITOR

The three cats were enjoying a little time in the late afternoon sunshine. They knew they needed to enjoy that warmth while they could, since they knew it was almost time for the cold weather to set in. They had recently heard some talk from Danny and the others at the fire station that the forecast is for an unusually cold winter with lots of snow and ice storms. The three cats were not concerned about it, since the firemen had just completed winterizing the three cats' cardboard box/home. They had acquired some good, heavy plastic that they used to completely wrap their home using heavy staples. This remodeling effort would help the three cats stay warm and dry during the storms this winter.

Tomcat opened his eyes from his quiet time in the sun to see a most unusual sight. On the fence across the alley sat a cat that he had never seen before. That cat was staring directly at Tomcat with cold, piercing blue eyes. Tomcat got the attention of Yellowcat and Alleycat, and they started discussing this newcomer. When "ole blue eyes" noticed that he had been seen, he turned his head and looked away as if to say, "I'm not interested in being friends with you guys."

That was okay with the three cats because it was now suppertime and they were all hungry. They decided to take today's catch from Fulton Street Fish Market out into the sunshine and enjoy a nice picnic meal. As they were enjoying the four nice fish that the fishermen had given them, suddenly "ole blue eyes" became interested, but never moved from his position on the fence. The three cats decided he must be hungry, too, so Alleycat took the best fish and laid it down at the fence directly below him. Well, that unfriendly cat knew exactly what to do. He ate his tasty meal, then when the three cats weren't watching, he disappeared. He left without even saying "thanks for the meal." The three cats decided he had jumped to the other side of the fence where there were lots of bushes. That was Mrs. Olsen's backyard and she only had a little parakeet in a cage hanging on her back porch sometimes. That would be a good, safe place for a cat to be. Mrs. Olsen would never be mean to any animal.

Now it was almost sunset and the three cats noticed a chill in the air. They went inside their cardboard box/ home thinking how warm they would be tonight. They would be sleeping on a nearly new, thick, soft blanket that Tomcat had found today in the dumpster behind Mrs. Pennymore's home. The coffee stain didn't bother them one bit, because they knew it would still be soft & warm.

The same scenario with the unfriendly visitor continued for several more days. (The free meal at supper time and each night was cooler than the night before.) The three cats started getting concerned and wondered how he would be able to survive the winter, since he probably had been a house cat all his life and not used to spending lots of time in the cold snow.

They decided to devise a plan to get Danny's attention that they needed help. So the plan to have Danny near their cardboard box/home at suppertime the next day worked. When Danny saw the cat on the fence they heard him mumble to himself. "Oh, that must be the Siamese cat that Officer O'Malley told us about." A lady had called and advised the police that she had been traveling through their town, stopped at a gas station, and after she left there she realized her cat had gone missing.

Next morning Officer O'Malley showed up in the alley with the nice lady. She jumped out of the car and started calling, "Symi - Symi, where are you? I've come to get you and take you home."

Symi, after hearing her voice, jumped over the fence swiftly, ran to the lady, climbed up the back of her coat and landed on top of the woolen cap on her head. The three cats thought, "That's a strange way to say hello to your owner." (It is well known that Siamese cats have odd ways and do strange things.)

The three cats were pleased that they had cared for "Symi" enough to provide his needs and plan a way to rescue him from having a cold uncomfortable winter.

When you think about it, isn't that what Jesus did for all of us? He loved us when we were unlovable, and came to us willing to provide our needs and rescue us from our unhealthy condition.

The snow began to fall just shortly before bedtime for the three cats. They fell asleep that night on their soft, thick, blanket inside their nice, cozy cardboard box/home.

Sweet dreams three cats!

THREE CATS AND THE CABBIE

Sometime during the fall last year the three cats, Alleycat, Tomcat and Yellowcat, were returning from grocery shopping in the dumpsters, in the alley behind Sterling Avenue. They noticed a taxicab parked in a drive-thru carport, located in an offset behind a nice home. They knew from talking to other older cats that an emergency room doctor had lived there in years past and had kept his car in the carport to be able to use it quickly to respond to a call from the ER, whenever he was on call. To see a cab parked there was unusual, but nothing to be alarmed about.

When they passed by an hour later they were surprised to see the same taxi still parked in the same place, so they checked it out. All cats notice things that are out of the ordinary, and they are inquisitive and like to check things out ..., it's another cat thing. They noted that the engine was idling, and the driver was slumped over the steering wheel as if asleep. The window was down on the driver's side, and they could hear the dispatcher's voice on the radio. The dispatcher was calling different cab numbers and giving them pickup orders at various addresses. They noticed he repeatedly called cab sixteen, but gave no address or other information. Then Tomcat said "Look at the number on the side of the cab – this is sixteen."

With this new information the three cats became concerned for the driver. Yellowcat jumped upon the windowsill where he hoped to awaken the driver, or at least see what might be wrong. He called down to the other two and told them the driver was breathing, but his head was turned in a funny way that looked uncomfortable to Yellowcat. As the radio continued to call number sixteen, the three cats discussed what they should do to get the cabdriver some help.

When they decided what to do, Alleycat stayed to watch over the cab and driver, while Tomcat and Yellowcat hurried to the police station just a few blocks away. When they got to the station they were happy to see the animal control officer's pickup truck was not there. They went to the garage entrance and found the big overhead doors open, as a couple of mechanics worked under the hood of one of the squad cars. They waited until someone opened the door connecting to the offices and quickly shot through the briefly open door. They knew where Sergeant O'Malley's office was, since he had brought them all there for visits in the past. They found him in his office with the door open, as he worked with his monthly, moving violations and accident reports.

Sergeant O'Malley was surprised and happy to see the duo and wondered where their pal, Alleycat was. He jumped up and closed the door, thinking the animal control man or someone might be bothered by the cats being there. Tomcat jumped up on the desk and promptly jumped back down and went to the door and gently, but noticeably scratched the door and pushed his face against it. O'Malley just arranged his papers on the desk, got his hat and opened the door to lead his friends to his car in the garage. Not one of the three were concerned about anyone seeing this unlikely scene, as they had more important things to attend to. As the sergeant got into his cruiser, the two cats ran purposefully to the curb and waited for him. When the big police cruiser started to the street, the two cats sped towards their destination with their tails straight up. When cats want to be noticed, they do this.

When they arrived back where Alleycat was watching the cab and driver, Sergeant O'Malley sprang into action. He checked the cabbie's pulse and moved him into a better position. Then he called the police dispatcher and requested an ambulance at the alley location. The ambulance arrived in just minutes and the EMT people checked the driver's vital signs and took him to the hospital. Before he left, O'Malley called the taxicab dispatcher and reported where cab sixteen could be found. Then O'Malley was petting the three cats and bragging to the other officers who had arrived, about "his" three cats and their public service deed. The dispatcher called on the radio to report the cab driver was found to be suffering from a diabetic coma, caused by his failing to remember to take his insulin shots on schedule. He said the man was out of danger and wanting to thank the three cats who had alerted the authorities of his problem. Tails held high ..., they strutted home.

THREE CATS AND THE BILLY GOAT

The three cats, Yellowcat, Tomcat and Alleycat were minding their own business, the business of taking a long catnap one warm, sunny afternoon in their cardboard box/home, when they were suddenly awakened by an unusual sound. The sound was of ripping and chewing, mingled with loud sounds of "BAAA – BAAA." They all three scurried outside to find a big, ole billy goat chewing a big mouthful of their house! That big ole ugly goat was surprised at their coming out of his box-lunch, but he didn't let that interrupt his repast (meal). The three cats were upset at this turn of events. Alleycat said "We gotta do something, he's gonna eat our whole house. The big, ole, dirty billy goat paid them little attention as he continued to bleat and eat.

They all three hissed and growled at the interloper, but he didn't pay them much mind, so Tomcat nipped him to get his attention. That proved to be very effective, as the goat wheeled around and lowered his head and pawed the gravel. This was a new thing for the cats, but they soon found out what the lowered head, pawing and bleating meant, as the goat charged at them to butt them with his horned head. He seemed to be targeting Yellowcat as he charged. Goats are very quick, but cats are quicker; as the goat charged fast, Yellowcat sprang straight up and landed on the goat's back. At first the goat was confused as to where Yellowcat had disappeared to, but when Yellowcat dug his claws in to maintain traction and balance, that ole, dumb goat figured it out. He tried to shake Yellowcat off and even ran under a low branch to try to rake him off, but Yellowcat held on firmly ... and painfully for the goat. When the goat wheeled around and ran at an even lower branch, Yellowcat expertly jumped from his goat perch to the tree limb.

Having discovered the cats to be faster (and smarter) than he was, the goat wanted nothing more to do with them and ran baaaing down the alley toward Cherry Street. Taking advantage of their new found control of the goat, the three cats began to herd him toward Sterling Avenue, where they hoped to get Mrs. Pennyrich's bulldog, Brutus, to help them. Brutus was, of course, asleep in front of his doghouse, when the loud baaing of the billy goat awakened him. This insured that Brutus would be in a bad temper, and when he saw his three friends chasing that ole, dirty goat he wanted to enter into the fun. Mrs. Pennyrich doesn't know it, but the gardener helped Brutus dig a place under the big iron gate, near the east hinge. The gardener carefully keeps the decorative bush there pruned and trained to keep it his and Brutus' secret.

Brutus quickly (well, quickly for a forty pound bulldog anyway) crawled under the gate and joined in removing that ole goat from the fancy neighborhood. With the barking, growling bulldog running point, the four smaller critters were doing a good job of cleaning up the area. They pursued the horned animal down Sterling Avenue almost to Main Street where a traffic officer reported the strange sight, and the animal control officer came to join the race. The goat ran into a blind alley and the other four pursuing posse members stopped at the alley mouth. The animal control officer parked his vehicle and got out with a rope loop on a long pole and advanced toward the goat who was baaing and pawing the dirt, with his head lowered into butting position. When he charged, the officer quickly and expertly lowered the noose and snared the threatening billy goat. He then led the bad boy to the pickup and placed him in the confines of the cage there.

The crowd that had gathered to watch all clapped at the peaceful outcome, and the three cats and Brutus removed themselves before the officer took too much notice of them. As they moseyed back to Sterling Avenue, they all four agreed this was a good example of what the dogcatcher should be doing. Brutus even suggested the man could be referred to as a billy goat catcher. Brutus slipped back under the gate, and the three cats continued homeward, discussing how they could possibly repair the goat damage to their house. Later they heard the billy goat's owner claimed him at the city pound and returned him to his job of eating the weeds and bushes at the property where he belonged. The three cats were happy to know this, and they all three agreed they hope to not hear BAAA for a long time.

THREE CATS AND THE A.W.O.L. CANARY

The three cats, Tomcat, Alleycat, and Yellowcat, were returning to their cardboard box/ home from a good day's dumpster diving, grocery trip. As they approached their box behind the alley dumpster, they all three sensed there was something peculiar or odd there. They slowed their gait and the most daring, Tomcat, ventured ahead of the other two and looked inside and returned to give them the news. Tomcat told the other two that there was a bird in their house, and Alleycat groaned that he couldn't hold another bite, since he was too full of discarded pizza right now. Tomcat explained this was a very small bird, and Yellowcat said he was just like Alleycat, too stuffed to hold another bite, even a very little bite. Tomcat was a little miffed at his pals for interrupting him and told them to get their stomachs off their minds and listen. He then told them that the bird was someone's little pet canary and was asleep in their box. They all went in and were quiet, so as not to awaken the pretty little bird.

Next morning, the three cats were already awake when the little canary first stirred. When he saw the cats he was terrified, (birds are instinctively (naturally) afraid of cats). Although scared out of his wits, the small bird couldn't flee, because he had an injured foot and wing, so he just cowered, awaiting his terrible, supposed fate. The cats couldn't reassure their guest of their good intentions very well, since birds and cats don't have much chance to talk with one another. Alleycat got some old, crumbly cheese from their rations and offered it to the hapless bird. The little canary was very hungry, but it took some time to dawn on him that this scruffy cat was trying to help him. When he had pecked and eaten quite a bit of the cheese, the canary became sleepy and nestled up against Alleycat, his new buddy, and went sound asleep.

The next day, the three cats started using their social network of other cats to find help for their guest. From Fluffy they got a small packet of birdseed that Fluffy's mistress had for her two lovebirds and parakeets. From a backyard bird cage across the alley they borrowed some chunks of suet, and everywhere they spread the word that they were looking for the home of their yellow feathered pal. Several of their buddies expressed their reservations about cats keeping birds as house guests, but everyone joined in the spirit of being good Samaritans* to the little injured canary. Meanwhile, the injured foot and wing of the little, feathered friend were healing, and he was getting stronger too. They had a problem getting necessary water to the little patient at first, but a good friend on Piper Lane gave them a bath sponge her mistress "lost," when her trusted house cat borrowed it for a just cause. Yellowcat took the sponge to a dripping faucet nearby and returned with the now soaked sponge and laid it near the bird and pressed it with his forepaws to get plenty of water. They were all surprised the first time their recovering patient got into the puddle of water and took a good bird bath. Cats don't do that, by choice, ever.

One day soon a friendly house cat, who has roaming privileges, brought word that his family, (I almost said "owners," but we all know the adage "dogs have owners ... cats have staff") had lost their young canary when he escaped while the kids were cleaning his cage recently. Returning that little yellow outlaw was a complicated effort. Maybe we can explore that yarn in a future report.

*The story of the good Samaritan is told by Jesus in your Bible at Luke 10:25-37. Read it; it's a much better story than this one and has been repeated millions of times in the past twenty-one centuries without variance.

Can you draw a canary here using yellow pencil or crayon?

THREE CATS AND THE WATCH

Lots of things happen every day in Centerville that the three cats, Tomcat, Yellowcat and Alleycat, are not involved in, or aware of. One windy day last spring started with the three cats sleeping late because they stayed up late the night before watching television on the patio with their friend Brutus. Mrs. Pennyrich had asked the butler to leave it turned on for Brutus, and the cats joined him just as soon as the mistress had gone inside. This morning, the weather front the weatherman had been promising had arrived with vigor, and the northwest wind was strong and gusty. During the rush hour traffic there was a collision involving a small truck and two cars near where Main Street runs under the loop. By the time the three cats appeared on the scene, the traffic officers and emergency medical techs had taken care of the injured victims, taking the more serious cases to the hospital. The officers had taken the necessary measurements, photographs and witnesses' statements. The wrecker crews were hooking up what was left of the three vehicles and sweeping up the broken glass and dirt from the street. The three cats watched these activities from behind a bus stop kiosk that provided protection from the strong wind.

The last young, wrecker driver had his tow hooked up and pulled out of the traffic lanes and was busy sweeping the pavement clean. He was interrupted by calls on his radio in the wrecker. The boss wanted to know the color of the Cadillac he was bringing to the impound. Then the manager wanted some information missing on his time sheet. Then the dispatcher called to ask how much longer he would be there at the scene. To this last question he told them the rest of the day, if they continued to interrupt his work. With all these interruptions and needing to hurry into the street during cycles of the traffic lights, he was somewhat frustrated and hurried. A brief opening in the cloud cover sent bright sunlight over the area, and he could only see a few sparkling glass shards reflecting the sunlight. As his radio called his number again, he decided that the street was clean enough and taking his broom and scoop, he climbed into the cab and thankfully closed the door on the howling wind outside.

After the wrecker left with the last vehicle, the three cats were studying the traffic flow to decide when to make their dash across the street to the other side in safety. When the time was right, and being mindful of the few remaining pieces of glass, they made their move. When Tomcat and Yellowcat were safe on the sidewalk, they realized Alleycat was not with them. They looked back and saw him stopped near the traffic island, doing something with both front paws on the pavement. Then the traffic began moving, and they couldn't see their pal anymore. The traffic was fast and thick as the drivers maneuvered their powerful vehicles. The two safe cats were worried for their friend's safety. When the lights stopped the flow of cars and trucks, there was Alleycat, safe on the concrete island. As they watched he looked both ways and serenely, with his tail straight up, sauntered to the walk where they waited. As he came closer, they could see he had a glittering something, dangling from his mouth.

That something retrieved from the street by Alleycat, was a diamond-encrusted, eighteen carat, pinkish, gold lady's wristwatch from one of the most exclusive Swiss watchmakers. Of course it was almost worthless to the three cats, since they have a natural, built-in sense of time and can't wear a watch on their wrists anyway. On the other hand however, they knew the pretty, little watch had great value to its owner. They discussed how to return the timepiece to its owner as they continued their trip to the fishing wharfs. Alleycat's danger wasn't over however. At the wharfs, one of the seamen noticed the watch hanging down from Alleycat's mouth and tried to snatch it away. The cats left there without any food for the first time ever and returned home safely with their expensive cargo.

It had been a harrowing day for the cats, so they rummaged in their stores of food and made-do with what they had on hand. They agreed to sleep on what to do about the watch tomorrow, as they went to sleep to the sound of the dying wind.

The next morning they found some almost fresh donuts in a paper sack, discarded in a nearby garbage can, so their day was off to a good start. Each one was focused on how to find the owner of the tiny watch with the big diamonds.

The three cats decided since there was only one lady involved in the three-way collision and she was taken to the hospital, their first move should be to go there. Today was a better day, and they set off for the hospital in high spirits to visit with Pugcat there. Pugcat is the pet of the hospital's official chaplain and is an overweight brown cat with a shortened nose and a get-outta-my-way attitude. When they arrived at the hospital, they went to the front door and timed their dash through the revolving door with their tails held high, so as to not get them caught under the turning doors. Once inside, they made their way to the small office of the chaplain, where they were happy to find Pugcat taking a catnap. They awoke him, and he was surprised and glad to see them. Surprised because cats aren't allowed there, and glad because he likes them and doesn't have the pleasure very often. Pugcat's ability to be there was due to a ruckus a few years ago, when the administrator questioned his being allowed inside, which led to a tussle with the chaplain. The matter was resolved when the local newspaper and radio and tv stations had a public poll, and people overwhelmingly voted for Pugcat's special exemption from the normal rules.

The three cats asked Pugcat if he could help them and he replied, "Can a pig eat slop?" He explained he would show them where they could wait, safely hidden in a closet, while he went with the chaplain on his ten o'clock rounds, which would include any patients admitted yesterday. When the chaplain returned to his office, the three visitors were already in the linen closet where they napped and waited. When the man returned with Pugcat, they were impatient to find what Pug had been able to find out for them. Finally, there was a brief phone call and the man left with Pug still there. Pug came to the closet and proudly announced, "The Widow Winters is in private room 214 and will be discharged tomorrow if her tests all come back positive."

That room number, 214, presented a problem since the 2 indicated the second floor. They made a plan and started on their happy mission. Since Pugcat knew every nook and cranny of the big building, he knew where he could hide his three buddies while he scouted ahead. His presence was accepted by staff members and ignored. When the coast was clear Pug would give a high-pitched hiss that humans can't hear, and the three aliens would scamper quickly to his new location and hide for the next step. They had good fortune and when they were hiding in sight of room 214, the nurse came out and left the door slightly ajar. Pug strolled down the hall from the hiding place as if he owned the entire hospital and entered the room to see if the patient was alone. When he gave the signal, a fast moving stream of three cats sped to the room.

The chaplain's phone rang, and he was told the patient in 214 had called and said his cat was there with three other cats. He said he would go calm her down and report back if she seemed to be hallucinating. When he arrived, a very excited, but clearly not hallucinating Mrs. Winters was sitting up in her bed with four cats and showing the man her watch she thought someone had stolen at the crash scene, or en route to the hospital while she was unconscious. She was happy to have the people vindicated, but was perplexed as to how Pug's friends had come into possession of the special watch her late husband purchased for her in a Bern, Switzerland, boutique. When she posed this question to the man of cloth he chuckled and told her, "You know what we Christians say; The Lord moves in mysterious ways His wonders to perform."*

The celebrating group were interrupted by a med nurse, who could not believe the zoo-like scene in the room. The chaplain explained that Pug was just there with some good friends of his and Mrs. Winter's and suggested we needn't get the administrator and the media involved. With this, he ushered the friends out a back door into the parking lot, where three nice looking, happy cats looked perfectly normal.

The only problem now is Alleycat spends a lot of time checking out any glittering object he sees everywhere they go!

* This is not Scripture, but is widely said since many verses in the Bible combine to affirm it.

Draw a Lady's gold watch here using gold or pink and diamonds made with white or silver colors.

THREE CATS AND THE LIGHTNING STORM

One summer night the three cats, Alleycat, Tomcat, and Yellowcat, were asleep at home in their cardboard box when they were awakened by distant thunder and flashes of lightning to the north of them. Soon the wind began to pick up, and the thunder was closer and more frequent. Alleycat was scared by the weather and the possibility that they might be struck by a bolt of lightning. Tomcat and Yellowcat tried to assure him that there was very little chance of their being struck, since they were neither on high ground, nor under a tall tree. It began to rain, and they all three shared a concern about their cardboard box not being able to withstand much water. Cats don't like to get wet; well the ocelot cat in South America likes to frolic in the water, but these are not ocelots. The

garbage truck men had laid an old discarded, card table top, on top of their box recently, and they hoped its plastic surface would keep most of the rain from soaking their cardboard box/ home.

When it seemed as if the thunder could get no louder, there came a crash like two trucks colliding, and the world turned bright-bright, bluish brilliant for a second. The dumpster next to their box moved, and the lid squeaked as if being opened. When the impossibly loud crash went away all three of them had a ringing sound in their ears and couldn't hear one another very well. The rain was still coming down like a waterfall, but the wind was tapering off. It was very dark, and when Yellowcat opened the flap door he could see two things. One – all the lights in the neighborhood were out and two – the big transformer at the end of the alley was afire with flames shooting up high and lots of smoke billowing into the darkness. As he was reporting this, Tomcat reported water coming on the floor from the side bordered by the fence, behind their box. They all three crowded atop some old rags and stuff to try to keep their feet dry.

Before the water problem became critical, they heard the siren and loud engine sound of the fire department's truck arriving at the transformer fire. While the firemen were occupied dousing the fire on the pole, the three cats were occupied finding a dry place, the elevated cab of ladder truck No. 5. Since their feet were already wet, they disregarded the shallow water flowing in the alley and made a beeline to the truck. Each one very quickly leaped to the running board and seemed to bounce like a rubber ball into the floorboard of the truck. It was dry and warm there, and they each one shook their feet and licked their paws to remove the offending water.

When the firefighters finished their assignment and stowed their equipment, they discovered the three cats in the cab and laughed as they recognized them as having visited many times at the station, where the people had fed and petted them. When the crew backed the big ladder truck into its parking spot, they invited the three cats to come into the living quarters, where they fixed them a nice bed of clean, dry mop heads and polishing rags.

Next morning, the cook fixed some scrambled eggs and sausage for the three cats who ate in the dining area, in a corner on the floor, as the men ate at the table. Since they knew where the three cats lived, they took them there when they had official business in the area and even took a new, sturdy box to replace the old, soaked one, which they discarded in the dumpster. They placed an old wood pallet under the new box and re-affixed the card table on top. The three cats watched with interest as the team did all this and knew it was going to be a nice improvement when they saw the men fold up an old, ragged quilt to the exact size to give the cats a wall-to-wall soft bed!

Ever since that summer night of lightning, when the three cats hear thunder, they go inside their box/home and remember to be thankful for the friendship and help from the firefighters. Alleycat puts his head under some of the bedding until the thunder stops. He says this helps a lot.

Can you draw the cats' box with the old ragged quilt in it? The box can be brown or tan and the quilt colored designs you like.

THREE CATS AND THE FOUL ODOR

The three cats were checking out the dumpster and garbage cans behind the VFW hall, on the night the people there have their monthly pizza fest. Cats don't have calendars or watches, but they have a good memory of what events follow other events. This was the night after the monthly shrimp dinner at the Fisherman's Wharf, where every free cat in town was in attendance. The pizza this night was fresh and tasty. When you've had nothing or very little to eat all day, any pizza is tasty. They were all three sharing a big piece of pepperoni pizza, when they spied several other cats coming their way, so they pulled the big morsel around behind the dumpster for more privacy.

While they were dining in their exclusive alcove, they all three noticed a strong, unpleasant smell which was not familiar to them. Cats all have a very well-developed sense of smell and can "follow their noses" to discover where any odor they are interested in is coming from. The three started sniffing between the dumpster and the alley fence for the source of the mystery smell. They were expecting to find something in a wrapping, or a box, or container of some sort. They found plenty of stuff to check out, but nothing seemed to contain the unappealing smell. Yellowcat put his nose close to the ground and worked his way toward the strongest smelling area. By the time he began to get closer, he had to stop because he was getting a little lightheaded and queasy in his stomach. Tomcat took the lead, where Yellowcat threw in the towel. He and Alleycat, working in relay shifts finally found the smell was coming from the surface of the alley. In fact, there was a crack in the pavement that had the bad-smelling gas coming out with force, making a spewing sound.

With their stomachs full of discarded pizza and Yellowcat feeling better for the fresh air, the three good friends made their way home to their cardboard box behind the dumpster, in "their" alley. Next morning, they discussed the thing they had discovered the night before and agreed that it might pose a problem for the people at the VFW hall, since it did make them woozy and sick feeling. They made the decision to see if they might be able to alert someone who could decide what action, if any, needed to be taken. First, they went to the police station to see if Sergeant O'Malley might be there, but the first thing they saw was the animal control officer's truck parked outside. Without discussing that, they continued the short distance to the fire station.

They found the crew there, busy polishing the big firetruck and doing other chores around the station. In an effort to get their attention, Alleycat jumped upon a shelf and got a pair of eyeglasses one of the men had just laid there. When this was noticed, the man reached to retrieve his glasses, but Alleycat playfully moved out of reach and with his pals, moved toward the open overhead door to the outside. All the team of firefighters found this amusing, except the owner of the glasses. As he moved faster to catch Alleycat, the cats moved just fast enough to stay out of his reach. In this manner, they led the owner of the glasses and another fireman toward their destination, the VFW hall. When the group of people and cats arrived in the alley there, the cats went behind the trash dumpster where Alleycat ceremoniously placed the purloined glasses near the fissure emitting the offensive odor. The firemen reacted immediately by calling on their radio to alert the station of the natural gas leak.

Things shifted into high gear, as the department vehicles and police cars began to arrive to move people out of the danger zone. They called the gas company, who dispatched a work crew to shut off the gas and repair the gas main. With all this, also came the newspaper and television reporters and camera crews. When the story developed about the three cat's involvement in the matter, the cameras searched them out, but all they got was a shot of the cats' tails held high as they departed. The three cats thought the dogcatcher might see the six o'clock news, so they left before the mayor showed up to congratulate everyone for removing a public danger from the community.

The three cats were delighted to see a happy ending to their problem and the city's safety.

THREE CATS AND THE RENDEZVOUS

All cats are curious by nature. That is to say, they notice anything unusual or different and have a natural desire to understand such things. A house cat entering a familiar room, will immediately take note of a new piece of furniture or change in curtains or anything someone may have left on the floor. There's even an old saying, "Curiosity killed the cat" which means sometimes needless inspection and investigation can result in time lost and bad outcomes. Anyway, even if it does kill the cat – don't they have nine lives, or is that just a brand of cat food? While we are digging into funny stuff, let's touch on that title word, rendezvous. It comes from the French language and means people meeting at a certain place for a specific reason. Now that we have gotten all that out of the way, let's get on with our story.

Cats don't have calendars or watches, as we have discussed before, but they do see when people do certain things at certain times. The three cats know, for instance, when the family behind the alley fence go shopping. They also know if the Martins take their pesky dog, Yap Yap, with them, because he sets up a lot of yapping when they leave him. When they take him, it is always a good time to jump up on the fence and then down to the nice lawn and explore what tidbits of dog food ole Yap Yap left for them. They also notice the day of the week when lots of families dress up and go to church and which churches sometimes have a fellowship meal after services. That's the day the three cats find some delicious scraps in the church garbage cans.

The three cats noticed that some nights before the big church day, two cars rendezvoused in their alley, usually arriving only minutes apart. There were usually two men in each car, and they got out and talked in hushed tones while looking a lot at the ends of the alley. These men appeared to be up to no good. Once, when Yellowcat sneaked up close to them one of them cursed and tried to kick Yellowcat with his booted foot. When Yellowcat quickly moved to avert being kicked, the man pulled a long barreled handgun from his waist and tried to shoot Yellowcat. The three cats noted the gun's report was a muted "pfftt" sound, just louder than a kid's air gun. Where the bullet struck the alley surface, narrowly missing Yellowcat, it made a great amount of destruction. After this the three cats stayed out of sight, but saw the men exchange gym bags before leaving by different directions. These were young, carelessly dressed men driving very expensive, new cars and trucks. They talked in vile street lingo with lots of curse words. They seemed to always be in a hurry as if they were late for their next meeting.

The three cats discussed all these things a lot, especially after the episode with the big quiet gun. They were in agreement that these things needed to be brought to the attention of the authorities, so they went to the police station on the next Saturday afternoon. Of course they went to their old friend, Sergeant O'Malley there, and of course the good sergeant was happy to see them. Happy, but tied up in weekend reports, so when he detected that his feline friends wanted his cooperation in some manner, he called in his nephew. Timmy is in the police cadet program training to be a police officer when he is old enough. O'Malley instructed Timmy to go with his friends to see what they were up to.

The three cats were happy with this; and they gleefully led Timmy towards their alley just as the sun was setting. When they all arrived at the cardboard box behind the dumpster the cats showed Timmy to a comfortable seat atop a wooden crate the trash men had shoved behind the dumpster for later pickup. This placed the young man's head just barely even with the top of the dumpster. Tomcat playfully removed Timmy's police cap, but instead of running with it to start a game, he placed it in Timmy's lap. This puzzled Timmy so he used his handheld radio to report to the dispatcher and request his uncle's help in what to do. O'Malley told Timmy to play it by ear and that it seemed to him that Timmy was on stake-out duty to observe with the three cats whatever they were concerned about.

After a long wait of almost two hours with nothing of note happening, Timmy was thinking of his mother's cooking, and why was he sitting on a hard crate hunkered down behind a trash dumpster. Then things picked up as a high dollar SUV entered the alley and dowsed its lights and parked. Timmy muted the speaker on his radio and placed the ear bud in his right ear and called the dispatcher to report this unusual and suspicious looking event. The dispatcher instructed the zone squad car to move nearby, and the district supervisor started that way also. A few minutes later a big four door luxury pickup truck entered the alley from the other end and turned off its lights as it parked nose-to-nose with the SUV. As two men from each vehicle got out to talk, Timmy with his heart pounding, quietly reported all this for the other police to hear.

The district supervisor instructed the officers nearest to the scene to synchronize entry from both ends of the alley with others giving backup. As the bad men were exchanging gym bags the police cars entered the alley from different ends at the same time with their emergency lights blazing. The bad guys were completely surprised and offered no resistance as the officers took them into custody.

When the police checked the contents of the two gym bags they weren't surprised to find one full of illegal narcotics and the other stuffed with bundles of money. In the vehicles they discovered several guns including the big, ugly gun the bad guy used that was so quiet. The officer, who discovered this gun hidden under the front seat of the truck, exclaimed that he thought the federal enforcement people would be very interested in this illegal silencer equipped handgun.

Timmy completely forgot his mother's cooking as he involved himself in these exciting matters.

When his now off-duty uncle arrived with the on-duty commander, Timmy was hardly able to stand the pressure he was feeling from the almost unreal happenings. When the narcotic officers arrived to take custody of the gym bags, they called to the handcuffed thugs using their street names, showing that they knew each of the four baddies. As the tow trucks loaded the outlaw's vehicles to transport them to the police pound, one narc officer called to one of the perps. "Nice wheels Shiv, now you're gonna have a paddy wagon and prison bus to haul you for a few years."

There were lots of congratulations being exchanged among the various law enforcement people as the paddy wagon departed with the miscreants. There were also lots of thanks extended to others. The assistant chief, who arrived late, thanked the commander and everyone. The commander thanked the district supervisor and the rest. Sergeant O'Malley thanked his nephew and the crew. Timmy thanked and bragged on the three cats. The three cats were thankful when everyone left and peace and quiet returned to their alley. The citizens of the town could be thankful for the protection given to them by the dedicated members of their police and fire agencies.

The next Saturday night the three cats were able to sleep with sweet dreams, a long catnap.

THREE CATS AND HOPPY TOAD

The three cats, Yellowcat, Alleycat, and Tomcat, were having their usual summer problem with pesky houseflies. Those old flies were everywhere, buzzing, and landing on the cats whenever they were trying to get a nice catnap. The cats twitched their tails to make the pests leave, but they soon returned to bedevil the cats even more. Then the weather turned rainy for a few days. The rain collected in little pools in places like old automobile tires, watermelon rinds, discarded bowls and jars.

In a few days there were mosquito eggs deposited in these out-of-the-way places. These eggs hatched into larvae, then into thousands of mosquitoes everywhere. Flies are bothersome; mosquitoes are painful ..., and dangerous.

The three cats were down by the creek behind the big church building hoping to maybe catch a fish or two. They heard, from the grass near the creek a "ribbit – ribbit" sound they knew was coming from a frog or toad. Then, between ribbits they heard a sound like zzitt followed by a gurgling sound. They weren't familiar with this sound so they left off their fishing duties and quietly eased in the direction of the sounds to see what was happening. Cats are quite good at doing things very quietly. There they saw a big toad squatting on a flat rock. In a minute they saw him flick his long tongue to snare a perched mosquito, making that zzitt sound and gurgling as he swallowed it. Almost at once he repeated the feat with a mosquito which was flying by.

The cats resumed their fishing; their curiosity satisfied about the sounds coming from the rock-based toad's mosquitoing.* They kept thinking and discussing the toad's accuracy and range using his very long tongue to get his food. They also noticed there were very few mosquitoes, and no flies there where they were. One of them opined as how it would surely be nice to have a toad in their alley to cut down on the swarms of flies and mosquitoes there. The other two agreed, as they continued to look for fish for their supper. Cats don't have to get fish hooks at the store to go fishing. Our Creator equips all cats with excellent fish hooks on their paws.

The three cats slowly formed a plan and when they were ready to go home they went to the toad and gently induced him to hop along with them as they slowly started home. They found they could control which way he hopped by one nudging him with his nose, while the other two stood with enough room for him to hop. It was slow progress; and they had to be super careful when crossing streets, since ole Hoppy Toad wasn't as fast as cats usually are while crossing streets. One of them referred to him as "Hoppy" and the name stuck since it was descriptive of his mode of movement. They finally got home just as it was getting dark.

The three cats fixed Hoppy a nice wet place to bed down for the night near the door slit into their cardboard box/home. Toads like wet places to rest and sleep. Sometimes they make their own.

Soon the three tired cats were nodding off with catnaps to the sounds of ribbit – ribbit and zzitt – gurgle. Early the next morning Hoppy was so busy with the day's swarm of flies, he didn't have time to ribbit between zzitt – zzitt – gurgle. Soon it was noticeable there were almost no flies or mosquitoes in their box/home. Thus, started a few days respite from the flying pests that had caused so much trouble for the three cats. They knew Hoppy was enjoying the plentiful food supply as he served as their doorman, but they knew he was more at home down by the creek. so they escorted him back when the mosquito population tapered off.

In the days to come the three cats remembered fondly the relief Hoppy Toad had given them from the painful, pesky mosquitoes, and the still bothersome flies. Then, one night, soon after darkness fell, they heard the happy sound of ribbit – ribbit and saw Hoppy stationed at his old position outside their front door. They were delighted, and awakened next morning to the sounds of pesky flies becoming breakfast fare for their visiting friend, Hoppy.

* Teacher says mosquitoing is not a proper word, but we thought it fit nicely there; and teacher doesn't read this stuff anyway.

THREE CATS AND THE FIRE STATION BATHS

The three cats enjoy visiting the firefighters at the local fire station for several reasons. The people there always treat the three cats really nice, and they usually have some good food to share with their visitors. Firefighters use water to douse fires, and they use water to wash their trucks and equipment at the fire station. Cats don't like water except to drink when they are thirsty. A type of cat, ocelots, enjoy playing and frisking in water, but they live in South America. Here we are thinking of other kinds of cats – house cats like Yellowcat, Alleycat and Tomcat.

One warm day last summer the three cats were roaming the "jungles" of streets and alleys foraging for food, when they decided to visit the fire station in quest for something to eat. The firefighters were glad to see their three friends and didn't disappoint them because they gave them some leftovers from the kitchen. The three cats purred as they eagerly filled their stomachs, then found a nice, warm soft place to take an after-dinner catnap. The crew began to discuss their dinner guests and someone mentioned that the black and white cat, Tomcat, looked like a police squad car with his color pattern. Another

commented that the brindle colored cat, Yellowcat, looked like a miniature Bengal tiger. Then someone added that they didn't really know what color Alleycat was because he always had dumpster garbage staining his fur with colors of ketchup, mustard, gravy, mayonnaise, A-1 sauce and whatever else he contacted while dumpster diving for groceries.

These discussions led to their thinking they would like to give the three cats a nice, warm soapy bath to enhance (help) their appearances ..., and discover Alleycat's real, natural color. They knew this would be a major project, knowing all cats' aversion to water. One older member recalled some years earlier they had treated the three cats to some catnip, and how they enjoyed it. One was dispatched to the local pet supply store to get some catnip, being careful to get the same brand as earlier so the cats would recognize it.

When the three cats awoke, the conspirators had a large dishpan filled with warm, soapy water and selected Tomcat for their first victim, since Tom was the easiest-going of the trio. They gathered around and all joined in talking in soothing tones, while bragging on Tom for being such a good boy as they introduced him to the water slowly. Tomcat went along with the foolishness, as he kept an eye on the box of catnip leaves. They soon got him completely bathed and fluffed up using a large towel and a quiet hair dryer. Tomcat was really proud of himself as he began playing with the catnip and forgetting the hassle of the bath. Yellowcat, having watched with interest Tom's bath and reward, steeled himself and endured a similar process without becoming too worried. As Tomcat and Yellowcat were playing with the catnip, the people turned their combined attention and efforts to the remaining cat. Alleycat had mixed emotions in the matter. On one hand, he didn't like the idea of the bath, but on the other hand, he liked the people bragging on their nice kittys ..., and the other two seemed to be very happy when it was all over with ...

The laundry detail worked soothingly with this last cat, recognizing that he was the most high-strung and strong-willed of the three animals. They carefully rubbed warm, soapy water on his paws and bragged on him for not resisting. Soon they had Alleycat covered with lots of suds and were rubbing the worst spots in an effort to remove the various stains and colors from his thick fur coat.

One said he was trying to remove some stubborn ketchup stains while others were busy scrubbing black and yellow and white areas. Then they rinsed off all the soapsuds and realized much of what they had been trying to remove was Alleycat's natural colors. They recognized that he was a multi-colored cat – a calico cat! When they got him toweled off, blow-dried and fluffed up they beheld the most handsome cat of the day. They gave the cats the catnip to play with as a reward and fed them a nice repast and marveled at the enhanced appearance of the trio.

The next time they saw their three friends Yellowcat was still brindle-yellow, Tomcat looked like a miniature Holstein cow and Alleycat was again muckley-dunn colored with remains of ketchup, mustard and barbeque sauce.

Can you sketch a catsup bottle in red and a mustard jar in yellow?

THREE CATS AND THE UNEATEN CANARY

All cats are fond of catching and consuming fish, birds, and rodents, when they are not being supplied with Friskies, Nine Lives, and Meow Mix. All members of the feline (cat) family, from lions and tigers to tabby cats, do well in finding food in all circumstances. Even house cats, raised in the wild, are able to fend for themselves better than most other domesticated house pets. Even a well fed cat, with a full stomach will usually catch an unwary bird whenever the opportunity presents itself.

One wet, dreary day the three cats were returning from a successful food patrol, when they saw a small, yellow canary limping along dragging an injured wing. None of the three was the least bit hungry, and the tiny bird looked so pitiful they immediately wanted to give it some help. The little song bird was instinctively afraid of the cats and cowered in a corner expecting the very worst. When the worst-looking of the trio opened his mouth the canary's fears seemed to be proven, but the ferocious looking beast only gently closed his mouth in a protective manner and the little bird was swiftly and effortlessly transported to a safe, dry, and soft place out of the weather with the three good Samaritans. A mother cat can carry her kitten in her mouth over great distances without harming her little one. The story of the Good Samaritan is in the Bible in the New Testament Book of Luke at chapter ten. It's a better story than the one you are reading here.

The three cats treated their house guest with love and care while feeding him seeds and suet pieces from Otto's Meat Market. The seeds were from wild grass growing in the edges of the alleys and from the ground around the bird feeders in some of the area backyards. They could see the little bird was feeling better and able to hold his injured wing in its proper place. On the fourth day it was very evident that the canary was better because he chirped several times. Two days later he sang a few notes of melodious song.

The three cats were worried that when he was well enough to fly he might leave their box/home and be lost, not knowing how to return to his home. Cats don't have telephones or twitter accounts to communicate among themselves, but they do have "cat com" to get the word around. We have all heard these messages being relayed among the feline population. We cannot understand them, but we do hear them sometimes in the middle of the night when they wake us from sleep. That's the time you want to throw a shoe or something at the involved cat to make them shut up already. The three cats began to circulate a message about trying to find if any of their associates knew of some family, who was missing a canary. They received lots of wisecrack answers from other cats about eating birds, but not much helpful input related to their problem of finding their guest's home.

Then, one nice morning they had two visitors. One was an old friend from another neighborhood and a friend of his, who was a stranger to them. The stranger told them outside of their box that his family had a little yellow canary they called “Chiki” who flew out an open window, while his cage was being cleaned almost two weeks ago. He further said that the family was very upset about Chiki’s disappearance, especially a young special needs girl named Alma, who kept the pet bird in her room. When the three cats invited the stranger inside to see if he could identify their guest, he demurred saying Chiki was always fearful of him, and he didn’t want to scare him if it were, indeed, Chiki they were keeping.

This was solved by allowing him to peer inside through a small peephole they used to check on the welfare of their house guest from time to time. After observing the canary inside the box the cat excitedly announced this was Chiki. Then there developed the problem of how to return the little bird to his rightful place. No problem; the three cats returned the tiny visitor by carrying him in relays, with each carrying for a short distance. When they got there, Alma was with her older brother in the backyard. Yellowcat set the canary down on the grass and they all watched as he chirped and flew into the outstretched hand of his little mistress, who giggled in pure welcoming glee. The three cats returned home, having made several new friends.

THREE CATS AND ROMO AND JULIE

Once upon a time there was a beautiful young lady named Julie, who lived with her wealthy aunt, Ms. Moola Richway. Ms. Richway was Julie's guardian and keeper of Julie's inheritance left by her parents when they died in an accident. The will provided for her aunt to receive money from the estate until it was turned over to Julie whenever she married or became thirty-five years old, whichever occurred first. Aunt Moola didn't spend much time looking for a suitor for her sweet niece, Julie. Julie enjoyed school studies, music instruction, her flower garden, and her blue ribbon winning cat, Tizzi. She didn't pay the boys in her life too much attention ... at least not until their gardener's nephew, Romo, came along. Romo was just older than Julie and was somewhat shy and very handsome.

Julie noticed how hard Romo worked and how polite he was to everyone. He was neat about getting all the dirt off his shoes when he needed to come inside to do things helping his uncle in his work.

The three cats, Alleycat, Yellowcat, and Tomcat, had been buddies with Tizzi for years. The three enjoyed sharing stories of their exploits with Tizzi and hearing some of the funny things Tizzi had to relate about his life of leisure as an award winning show cat. Sometimes they brought some scraps of food from Mr. Otto's Meat Market or some fish from the fisherman's wharf. Tizzi shared the fancy food his mistress, Mrs. Richway, provided him with. They all swapped yarns and gossip from their own experiences. The mistress didn't really approve of the three cats, especially Alleycat, who wasn't always the neatest animal, but she tolerated their occasional presence since Tizzi and Julie both delighted in their visits.

While adjusting the curtains in Julie's room, (really just snooping) Moola found a message from Romo in Julie's inbox. It was an innocent reply to an earlier request from Julie for the loan of a book of poetry his mother had given him for his recent birthday. This discovery by the aunt led to a talk with Julie where Moola accused her niece of going behind her aunt's back and encouraging Romo's interest in her. She told her niece that she felt betrayed and told her there would be no supper for her that night.

Julie also felt betrayed, and misjudged. She sobbed herself to sleep after a long time.

Moola Richway set about nipping the problem in the bud. She told Romo's uncle not send his nephew inside whenever Julie was there. She forbade Julie from being in the garden, whenever the two gardeners were working there. She took away Julie's phones and laptop.

She stopped all forms of communications between the two young friends. These actions made Julie very sad, and Tizzi sensed it and told his pals, the three cats, all about it. When Julie began to lose her appetite, stop studying hard and lose interest in her music lessons, Tizzi was concerned. Moola seemed not to notice any of this as she dreamed up other, more severe ways to keep Julie and Romo apart.

Tizzi told his buddies, the three cats, about all these things, and how he wished he could do something-- anything, to help matters. Meanwhile, all these restrictions on Julie's freedom was bothering Romo a lot. The three cats watched from hiding as Romo tried to cast a small note he had written, up to Julie's second story window. When it fell back to the ground for the third time, Tomcat retrieved it and was returning it to Romo. Then he had a brilliant idea. As Romo watched in wonder of what was happening, Tomcat scurried to the trunk of the sturdy, old oak tree and swiftly climbed high up to a long limb extending almost to the roof. Tomcat easily jumped the remaining distance to the roof near Julie's window. He then went to the window and scratched on the screen and meowed. Cats are good at scampering, climbing, walking on tree limbs, scratching and meowing.

Of course, Julie opened the window and took the offered note from Tomcat. She giggled as she read the note and patted Tomcat's head and caressed his fur. Tomcat just basked in the good feeling from helping out, and patiently awaited her return note to Romo. Moola never discovered what went wrong with her censoring program and wondered why her pretty little niece had resumed eating and studying and practicing her music lessons. Romo's uncle didn't know for sure, and he never took time to share his suspicions with his employer. As they say ..., everyone lived happily ever after.

THREE CATS AND THE RAGGEDY ANN DOLL

The three cats were enjoying a nice catnap in their cardboard box/home late one winter day when their sleep was rudely interrupted by the loud voices of some school boys in their alley. These youngsters were laughing and scuffling as they came down the alleyway. The three cats were alert, but remained in the box, so the ruffians wouldn't know they were there. They were prepared to abandon the box, if necessary, but kept still and quiet. As the kids came closer to the dumpster in front of the cats' box, the cats heard something tossed into it. When the rowdy group had made their way out of the alley, Yellowcat eased outside and jumped up to see what had been thrown into the dumpster. At first he thought it was a little baby girl, but closer examination showed it was a doll – a Raggedy Ann doll. With the help of his two pals, they were able to get the doll out of the trash dumpster and into their cardboard box/home.

Later that night the three discussed this unusual event. They agreed that none of the gang of boys owned the doll, and speculated on who the rightful owner might be. They surmised the owner might be a young girl, who lived somewhere in the Pinehurst Addition, since the doll was of simple but sturdy construction. They all thought the doll wasn't as expensive looking as the ones they often observed the girls on Sterling Street playing with. Next day they went together to the Pinehurst community and talked to the few cat friends they were acquainted with there. They were told of a girl, who had a Raggedy Ann doll. They then went there and waited in a big tree overlooking the backyard, which contained a well decorated playhouse. The elevation of the tree was good for them, but even more importantly it afforded safety from the many stray dogs roaming in the area. Not too long after they got comfortable, the little girl came from the sliding glass door of the home into the backyard. She had another girl about her age with her, and both of them had Raggedy Ann dolls in their hands.

The following day the weather was cold and rainy, turning into sleet after noontime, so the cats stayed home with their Raggedy Ann doll. It was trash truck day in their alley, so they were thankful they had retrieved the doll earlier and saved it from being hauled to the landfill. Landfills used to be called garbage dumps, but refined people renamed them – they still look and smell about the same.

When the weather improved a few days later, the three cats had a visitor, an older, gray cat, who told them he lived in Pinehurst and had heard of their visit there a few days earlier. He also told them the twin sisters living next door to him received Raggedy Ann dolls for their birthday a few weeks ago. He said some young punks from the nearby detention school unit had recently jumped over a fence and took one of the twins' doll. When he got a look at the doll in the cardboard house, he was delighted and said it was the one the brats had taken from the twins. This made everybody very happy, but they were faced with the problem of getting the twins there to get their doll, or getting the doll delivered to the twins. The elderly visitor told them to leave it up to him, and that he would plan to return tomorrow or the next day to get the doll.

The old, gray cat didn't explain his plans further, but left after the three cats shared some scraps of German sausage from Otto's with him. The following day when they returned home from helping clean up the fisherman's wharf, they were surprised and dismayed to see a very large sheepdog nonchalantly lying at the end of their dumpster. (well, it's the city's dumpster, but the cats think of it as theirs.) The big, ole dog seemed friendly as he rolled his eyes to greet them, thus saving the energy to move his massive head. Then things became more clear, as the elderly, gray cat emerged from their house and said he was ready, with his sheepdog friend, to return the doll to the twin, who was grieving at her loss. With this, the cats pulled the doll from their house, and the big, long haired dog gently picked it up with his mouth. Motorists and passerbys were treated to a most unusual sight as a large dog with a Raggedy Ann doll in his mouth was seen escorted by four cats headed toward the Pinehurst Addition. The animals were as happy as the human observers were confounded and amused.

That night twin girls and twin Raggedy Ann dolls were very happy together again.

THREE CATS AND THE CATERPILLAR

The three cats were returning home from a good fishing trip at the creek behind the big church.

They all three had really full stomachs and were taking their own sweet time. They stopped under a small tree with leafy limbs low to the ground, to rest a few minutes in the cool shade the tree afforded.

Back near the edge of the alley, where it joined the border fence were some broadleafed plants the cats had heard the city work crews call milkweeds, as they left them growing while clearing out other plants.

There, on one of those leaves was a colorful, caterpillar worm busily eating the leaf at the edges. The cats thought how nice it would be, to be able to eat vegetation that grows everywhere, until Yellowcat asked how that would work out during the winter months, when most vegetation isn't available. After they rested a while the three cats resumed their journey home.

About a week or so later, the three cats were getting their fill of pizza scraps from the garbage cans behind the big church, when they decided to check to see if that caterpillar with the colorful, paint job had run out of leaves to eat. They found the big worm hanging from a stem of a leaf not far from where he was grazing earlier. He seemed to be asleep so the cats left him alone, saying to themselves that they would check on him next week, when they came to the area on a fishing trip again.

When the three cats were there the next time, the caterpillar had himself still hanging from the leaf stem, but he was slowly encasing himself in a sort of sack made from silk-like material he was making from the leaves he had been consuming earlier. When they next looked a while later, the big worm was completely inside the pod he had made, and was completely out of sight.

Early one morning some days later, the three cats were in the area and went by to see how their caterpillar was getting along inside his pod. They found the pod still attached to the stem where it was the last time they were there, but the head of the creature inside was struggling to come out of what was still left of the pod. Then they could see that what was coming out wasn't the caterpillar at all, but something else which was different. As they watched in amazement, they saw a slowly emerging insect of a different nature from the big worm of earlier visits.

They were spellbound as they watched in awe, as the creature slowly morphed into a beautiful butterfly – a beautiful Monarch butterfly. The three cats had seen these most beautiful of all butterflies many times over the years. They had seen them gather in great masses in the fall of the years and migrate south in clouds of orange hues. They never knew where the pretty creatures went, but now they knew where they came from. Those stunningly pretty, flitting – flying butterflies come from those rather ugly, big worms hatched from tiny, orange-colored eggs their mothers deposit on the leaves of the common looking milkweed plants. Having learned this lesson from nature, the three cats decided to stop by the fire station for a short visit on their way home to their cardboard box/home for a good long catnap.

****

If you are interested in the unique lives of the Monarch butterflies you can find lots of interesting information by checking Google or an encyclopedia. In fact, there are books that recount the way these unusual insects migrate every fall from their birthplaces to Mexico and return every spring. The three cats can't check these sources like we can, but they had an opportunity to see it up close and personal in a way few humans ever have. Isn't it amazing the many ways nature (God, really) arranges for all living creatures to reproduce and keep their species alive for generations in His beautiful world? Wouldn't it be stupid and disrespectful on our part to do anything that might upset or interfere with the normal life cycles of His creation?

Hope you enjoyed this three cat tail – er, tale. (The authors.)

THREE CATS UP THE CREEK TREK

There are old sayings, "Up the creek" and "Up the creek without a paddle" which mean out of luck – having big problems. This little essay isn't about such troubles; it's about a trip the three cats took one week last summer. They were again down by the creek behind the big church building doing a little fishing. As they were attending to their fish catching, they were as usual, talking about other things of interest to all three of them.

This little creek continues down to join the big river, not too many miles from where the three cats do their fishing and exploring. Once a few years ago, they had roamed down creek to where the big river was joined, and they had heard of even further where the big river emptied into the bay connected to the ocean. They had never been there themselves, but heard from others who had ventured that far. This day the conversation turned to wondering where the creek started somewhere in the rising terrain and hills to the north. They decided they would start tomorrow morning and explore the creek to find its origin.

The next morning the weather was warm and cloudless, and the three cats were down at the creek ready to explore. They were as well prepared as they could be, since cats don't carry much stuff with them when traveling. They started walking along "their" side of the creek, as far as the fence that comes all the way past the creek's edge. Fences keep cows and horses and sheep and goats restricted, but cats usually don't pay fences too much mind. Since this particular barbed wire fence extended into the creek, they simply crawled under the bottom strand and continued their steady movements up the creek bank, as it wound its way up the slight grade toward the trees they could see in the distance.

About noon, they stopped at a place where the main current of the creek was away from the bank, as a big pool of still water was there and was pretty full of small, perch type fish. These were easy to catch without the cats needing to get very wet, so they had a nice meal and found a shady place under a big weeping willow with nice, soft grass. It was a perfect place for a good, afternoon catnap.

When they stirred from their catnaps, they were refreshed and in good spirits to continue their trip toward wherever the creek started. They came to other fences from time to time, but none of those presented any problem for the cats. They even came to a county road, which had a low bridge allowing cars to cross the creek. They used this bridge to cross the creek and see what things looked like over there. After a short sojourn there, they decided they preferred "their" side, so they backtracked to the bridge and continued their journey. As they moved through tall grass areas, they found lots of grasshoppers and other cat food. The creek with its clear, cool water was ever near when they became thirsty.

As the sun was becoming low in the west, they came upon several meadowlarks feeding on grass seeds and had two for supper (not grass seeds). With full stomachs, the three cats began to be on the lookout for a good place to spend the night. Just as dusk was coming on, they found a place where there was an overhanging large rock with plenty of soft moss covering the ground underneath. Since no one else was camping there, the three assumed it was meant for their enjoyment. They all curled up together and were asleep before the moon came up in the east.

Next morning the three cats were up and ready to go before sunup. They enjoyed their first-ever crayfish breakfast at the creek bank and resumed their trek up-creek. The going was somewhat slower now as the pastures and fields of yesterday, gave way to unimproved areas of unfenced woodland with lots of vines and underbrush. They could see that the terrain across the creek was still in fields and pastures with herds of grazing cattle and a few horses. There were no roads crossing the creek anymore, so they were finding it more work to fend their way. Then they came upon something they had never seen. There ahead of them was a dam extending completely across the creek! This was not a manmade dam, but one made by beavers, who were everywhere, working like – well, like beavers. These furry animals were somewhat like cats, except bigger and with broad, flat tails, and they loved the water! They swam like fish and communicated by slapping their flat tails on the ground.

The beavers stopped their work to look at the unlikely appearance of three city cats, but they showed no fear of their dry land cousins, nor any threat to them. The three cats took advantage of the beaver's dam to cross to the more civilized side of the creek. They saw the dam was constructed of logs and tree limbs the beavers had expertly arranged with mud to make a watertight construction, similar to their houses they lived in.

This other side of the creek afforded much better walking, and the three cats even playfully raced ahead of one another, as they continued their northward journey. They once saw two big bobcats chasing after a rabbit, and were impressed at the size and speed of the cats. Then, late in the afternoon, they saw a big mama cougar with two young kittens, who were bigger than any of the three cats. When they saw these larger, untamed cats, the three would practice their inborn instinct to hunker down and stay very still. Looking at the much larger cats, they wondered what they might eat in addition to rabbits, but they didn't want to find out the hard way. They began to look for somewhere safe to spend the night..., somewhere safe from giant cats and other dangers. They found a small cave with a dry, sandy floor with a small opening and deep enough to allow them to sleep out of reach from the biggest cats (at least the biggest they had seen so far).

Next morning it was warm inside their little cave, but when they went outside they found it to be pretty cool, with a cold north wind. They agreed to stay inside until the sun had time to warm things up a bit. Around midmorning, they ventured out and went to the creek to catch breakfast and resumed their exploring up-creek. They were used to seeing big cows in the pastures, but this morning they saw a bigger animal with something carried in its horns. They had never seen a moose before and laughed at its appearance with the funny looking horns making him look very top-heavy. The three cats didn't stop for their usual catnap after lunch, since they had slept late. That evening they came to a large pool of water that was bubbling with gushing water from the bottom. When they circled around this pool, they found no more creek! Eureka! This was the source of their creek, the headwater they had been looking for.

They were so happy to find this that they almost missed hearing some loud splashing and animals making unusual sounds on the other side of the pool. When they noticed this and moved to where they could observe the commotion, they saw their first ever otters. At first they supposed these animals were some kind of beavers, but could see they didn't have broad, flat tails. The otters were sliding down a mud chute they had fashioned where the bank was several feet high from the grass down to the water's surface. They were playfully competing to see who could get to the slide first and make the biggest splash entering into the pool. The three cats were almost ... I said almost ... persuaded to join the otters in their game. The otters didn't pay the three cats much mind; they may have assumed they were mountain lion kittens and wondered where their mama was.

The three cats liked it here at the big spring, watching the playful otters and eating perch and crayfish, but resolved to start their return trip home tomorrow. They found a good place to spend the night in safety and curled up for a good night's sleep. They were awakened several times as different animals came to the pool for water, since there was scant water uphill from this place.

Next morning the three adventurers were elated to be heading back home to more of the things they were used to, fewer surprises, and different things to experience. They were looking forward to getting back to their alley and their cardboard box/home, where the cats were all pretty well the same size. And it would be downhill all the way.

THREE CATS AND THE MOTHER HEN

Alleycat, Tomcat, and Yellowcat were returning from a trip to Otto's Meat Market and were almost home to their cardboard box/ home when they stopped to watch a man who was busy rearranging some large cages of chickens on his truck. As they observed, one of the cages slipped and fell to the street and the door flew open. Several chickens escaped, and the man was busily trying to round them up back into the metal cage. One brown hen quickly evaded the man's efforts and ran into the three cats' alley. Before the man could get the other chickens back into the cage, the brown hen ducked behind the big dumpster and straight into the three cats' cardboard box. The man came hurriedly down the alley,

but he didn't give that old box a second look. In a few minutes, he returned driving the truck, looking but not seeing any indication of where his hen might be.

The three cats had seen the hen go into their box/home and discussed how they could help her. Chickens don't really trust cats to help them, and for good, historic reasons. The three cats decided to offer the hen a place to stay in another cardboard box located next to theirs that was vacant, since their cousin, Bobbycat had returned to his regular home in the country. Tomcat went to the flap door of their box and made small meowing sounds as he came into the hen's view. She was fearful of Tomcat, but he made no threatening move as he curled up in a far corner. The other two cats hurried to a nearby backyard, where the people kept a well-stocked bird feeder. Yellowcat took a plastic bowl and filled it with "borrowed" bird seeds, and he and Alleycat brought it to their box and gently pushed it in front of the brown hen. She was wary of these cats and their strange antics, but she was also very hungry, since she had nothing to eat since yesterday morning.

When the hen started pecking seeds from the bowl, the cats slowly moved it in small steps to the other box. The chicken took steps as needed to keep the food where she could eat from the bowl. In just a few minutes she, without really noticing, was eating inside her new box/home. The cats had a sardine tin half full of rainwater, so they got it positioned beside the bowl of seeds. They didn't have to draw the hen a picture showing her what that was for, and she ate and drank just like she was at home there. As the cats continued to help the hen and take care of her safety, she became more and more relaxed in their presence. She even allowed one or another of them to sleep in "her" cardboard box, as she felt safer when they were close by. The hen had never been in a city venue (setting) before and wasn't used to the many sounds and sights there. When she ventured out of the box to forage in the grass lining the alley for seeds and bugs, she felt more secure if one or more of her friends were there.

Then ... she became more guarded and selective about the cats' close presence, because she had a nice brown egg in her nest in her box. She became very careful that nothing endanger that egg. Soon there were more of those little brown eggs, until she had seven there in her nest. She began to sit on those eggs and went outside less and less. The three cats didn't understand these changes in their guest, but catered to her by bringing food and water to her. This went on for quite a while and the three discussed it among themselves, wondering what, exactly, was going on.

Then, one morning while the other two cats were gone dumpster diving for breakfast, Yellowcat was home on what they called "biddy watch," keeping an eye on the hen, when he heard an unusual sound for the first time. The new sound was a cheeping sound he had never experienced before. Yellowcat started around his box to see what was making that new sound, but the hen made an angry sounding clucking that stopped him. He was stopped ..., but not blinded, there close to the hen was a little baby chick. A fluffy-downed, little yellow, baby chicken! This was very exciting to Yellowcat, and he could barely wait to tell the other two. By that time there were two more new chicks to tell about. When all seven were hatched out they soon made quite a sight with their mother. The three cats were proud as they could be, but were concerned for the little newcomers' safety. They arranged with a country cousin to get his farmer friend to come and get the eight chickens and take them to the country, where they could roam freely and safely with lots of other chickens. It became much quieter in the three cats alley, and they promised themselves to visit that big, poultry farm soon.

THREE CATS AND THE FISHING BOAT

The three cats were down at the wharf where the fishing boats unload their day's catch for the Fulton Street Fish Market. As always, some of the crew tossed small fish to the three hungry cats until they were no longer hungry. In fact, they were so stuffed they didn't much relish the thought of having to make the long trip home and were looking for somewhere to take a nice catnap while their food digested a bit. The crew from one of the boats had gone ashore after they got unloaded, and the gangplank was still in place to allow loading and unloading of the boat. The three cats scampered aboard the fishing vessel and down into the crew's quarters, where they found a nice clothes hamper open with nice soft clothing that beckoned them to curl up for a spell. The gentle rocking of the boat quickly lulled the three into sweet dreams.

With all the different sounds of ropes rubbing, pulleys turning, and things clanking, as the boat rode the small waves at the dock, the three cats failed to hear the crewmen, who boarded to move the boat. When they awoke and looked, the boat was being tied up to the mooring cable in the turning basin with the other overstayers. A pilot boat picked up the crewmen to go ashore, and the three cats were marooned for the night in the middle of the basin ... alone.

Next morning the crew was dropped off at the boat by a water taxi. The three cats stayed out of sight awaiting a chance to get ashore. The crew began to work with their nets, as the boat was brought to the fuel pump and the ice machine. Filled with the needs for their trip to the fishing grounds, the captain steered the boat toward the open sea. At the same time the three cats were also filled – filled with fear and foreboding because they weren't supposed to be there and the wave-induced motion of the boat was already making them a little woozy.

They had intended to just invite themselves aboard for a catnap, but circumstances had presented them with tickets to a two or three day fishing trip in the wave-tossed open ocean. A little before noonday the ship's cook was preparing lunch and the three cats could smell the aromas from his cooking from their hiding place. Usually, smelling food cooking made them hungry, but this time it made them feel more like upchucking than eating. About midafternoon one of the crew moved some of the clothing in the hamper looking for something he wanted. He found some things he didn't want, three things he didn't want, in fact.

The crewman reported his discovery to the captain. The captain was not happy to hear it. The crew discussed the matter at the evening meal and some jokingly suggested making the stowaways "walk the plank" as punishment for stowing away on the boat. The cabin boy, with the captain's okay fixed the three cats a good place away from the working areas to stay. When he offered them some food, no one was interested. Alleycat said he would probably be very hungry if things would stop moving for even a few minutes.

For the next two days and nights the crew was manning the nets and unloading lots of good fish into the ice hold. They spilled the nets onto the culling table where they discarded unwanted fish back into the ocean, before dumping the good stuff into that ice hold. The three cats had never even imagined there were so many fish of so many different kinds in the whole world. There were big fish and little fish and in-between sized fish everywhere. On the second night, the cabin boy brought the three cats some chicken broth and they were all three able to eat some and drink some fresh water he offered. Tomcat told the other two that he had found a way to overcome the constant motion of the boat. He said all you have to do is lift one foot and stand on three, and then lift another foot to stand on two. Then, he said you must lift one more foot while balancing on the only one remaining. The last and most important thing is to lift that last leg from the deck, and then you are removed from the motion of the boat.

When the fishing boat was filled with a good catch of valuable fish, the nets were rolled up and the boat turned to a heading back to port. When they finally arrived back home, the first ones off were the three cats, and they didn't want a take-home container of fish and chips.

Can you draw two fish? Remember to put scales on them.

THREE CATS GET STREET LEGAL

When hot rod enthusiasts build a car for racing or just for a show car; and if their creation doesn't have fenders, lights, normal doors, etc. it is termed as "not street legal." In other words, not legal to operate on public streets. If they should take such a vehicle and add the items necessary to license their auto, they then refer to it as "street legal." Tomcat and Yellowcat had in earlier times been street legal, licensed with the city and wore tags issued by the veterinary doctor's office.

Since they had been living for several years *on the streets* there had been no way for them to get their shots and tags.

After the three cats had been involved in aiding the police and fire departments in recent times, the chiefs of those departments had talked about having an awards function of some kind to bring the cat's community services to public attention. It seemed to these two department heads to be desirable to have the heroes' papers in order before any such event. Not wanting to disturb the cats at home, the officials agreed to just wait until they presented themselves at the fire station or police precinct.

Sure enough, the three wandered into the fire station soon thereafter and the crew with orders already issued, loaded up the three unwary cats into the chief's official vehicle and delivered them to the animal clinic nearby. The three cats trusted the firemen completely, based on lifetime experiences with that group of reliable, loving people. When the doctor got his needle in hand, their trust wavered somewhat. The shots and examinations were quickly completed and the nurse gave each cat a bit of catnip when she affixed their shiny new tags.

There were a few things affected by these changes. The three cats had a new home address on their tags, City Fire Station #3. There was no need now for them to get scarce whenever the animal control officer's truck came into view. The cats now needed to take care that the small chain securing their tags didn't become snagged on anything. They had to reassure their untagged friends that their new status in no way was to interfere with their old friendships. All-in-all the three cats were happy and thankful to the city employees, who went to the trouble to get them all legit. Speaking of city employees, the animal control officer said he was really glad the three cats got their tags. Glad he can stop looking the other way when he sees them trying to hide from him, whenever he drives down their alley. Glad the officers at the precinct station can quit stuffing the cats into closets and desk drawers, whenever he stops by for coffee.

The mayor said he was glad the television camera crews can now stop editing the three cats out of the six-o'clock news, every time they are mentioned because of the many good deeds they perform.

His Honor did say he hoped someone would clean the ketchup, mayo and mustard off "that nice calico cat" before any official camera shots. There was even some discussion around city hall about naming the three cats as the official feline representatives for the city. This was somewhat talked down by the local kennel club people, since there had never been any honors considered for the dogs in the town.

The three cats discussed their new-found status among themselves and agreed that they needed to be careful that this not go to their heads too much. After all, they knew of too many examples of cats, who had pretty high opinions of themselves. They thought it was enough that many people already thought of them as "their cats." Otto, at the meat market, had called them his cats for years. The members of the big church thought of them as theirs. The folks at the VFW called them "our cats," and the people at the fire and police stations had "owned" them forever.

So really, nothing had changed. The rest of the townspeople now shared in the sponsorship of the three cats, now that they were licensed. The three cats knew, of course, that it was really the other way around. It was they, who owned the entire city, since they were now street legal!

Can you draw a pet tag? Remember it needs a small hole near the edge for the beaded chain.

THREE SICK CATS

At first it was just the sniffles ..., Yellowcat just had a runny nose. Next day Yellowcat was having a little fever and some aching in the joints of the leg bones and didn't want to eat his share of the good stuff Alleycat found in the dumpster behind Sterling Street. By the third day, poor Yellowcat was miserable and didn't want to talk too much, or eat anything. Tomcat and Alleycat were very concerned for their pal, so Tomcat went to the fire station to get some help from their friends working there. The crew at the station were having a training session and watching a video on controlling fire in a setting with combustible contents. Tomcat didn't really want to interrupt the training session, but he felt it was important to get some help to Yellowcat ASAP, so he got everyone's attention by standing in the open door and letting out a really blood-curdling yowl. When everyone turned to see what was happening, Tomcat fell on the floor and began rolling over as if in great pain. When the first person came to help him, he ran a crazy pattern out into the yard and had another rolling, meooowing fit. By this time everyone was into seeing what was the matter.

Pretty soon Tomcat had two of the younger guys still trying to see what was wrong, as they neared the cardboard box behind the trash dumpster, where the three cats live. As soon as they saw poor Yellowcat they realized, who was really sick and called for their EMT unit to come assist them. When they arrived, they wrapped Yellowcat in a blanket and transported him to the veterinarian, Doc. White, to get him checked out. Doc. White dropped what he was working on when he heard the ambulance whine into his clinic's driveway. Not many animals arrive at the vet's clinic in such manner. The EMTs delivered the blanket-wrapped Yellowcat who looked pretty bad, with his eyes mostly closed and no interest shown in his surroundings.

Doc. White had a grim look on his face as he checked Yellowcat's vitals. He asked the techs why they had waited so long in bringing the cat to him. They explained that they didn't know of the problem until the visit by Tomcat. When they described how Tomcat got them to follow him to the location where Yellowcat was sick, Doc. White wondered out loud if Tomcat was just putting on a show for them, or if he was perhaps affected with Yellowcat's illness also. While the doctor and nurse began an IV, while monitoring heart rate and respirations, he told the EMT guys, he would like to see the other cats as soon as they could arrange it.

The crew returned to the alley home of the three cats and loaded the two there into the ambulance and returned, quietly to the animal clinic. Doc. White checked the two and opined that they had early stage indications that they were suffering from the same malady, probably contracted from exposure to Yellowcat. He gave both cats a shot of the same medication

Yellowcat had just received by IV. He told the medics that all three cats needed to be kept at the clinic overnight, with Yellowcat probably needing to be there for a few more days, since he was "rather critical" when admitted for medical attention.

Next day the EMT guys stopped by as previously arranged and took Alleycat and Tomcat back home and left them some dry cat food and some nice soft blanket scraps. The cats didn't feel like going looking for food, so this worked out really well.

Back at the animal clinic, Yellowcat began to feel better and take a little interest in his surroundings and start being picky about the food they brought him. When Doc. White finally said he could go home tomorrow, Yellowcat saved the city employees the trouble of returning him to his pals and their cardboard box/home. He waited calm as a cucumber curled up at Doc. White's feet until the janitorial staff left the back door open for a few minutes to take out the day's trash. Then – without so much as a thank you all – Yellowcat showed what a fine job the good doctor and the nurses had done. He quietly, but very quickly made a beeline for that opened back door and shot like an arrow for the alley. He was home before the janitors got through with their clean up duties.

Doc. White asked his wife, the bookkeeper, if she had the address in the alley behind the dumpster, so they could send the three cats a bill.

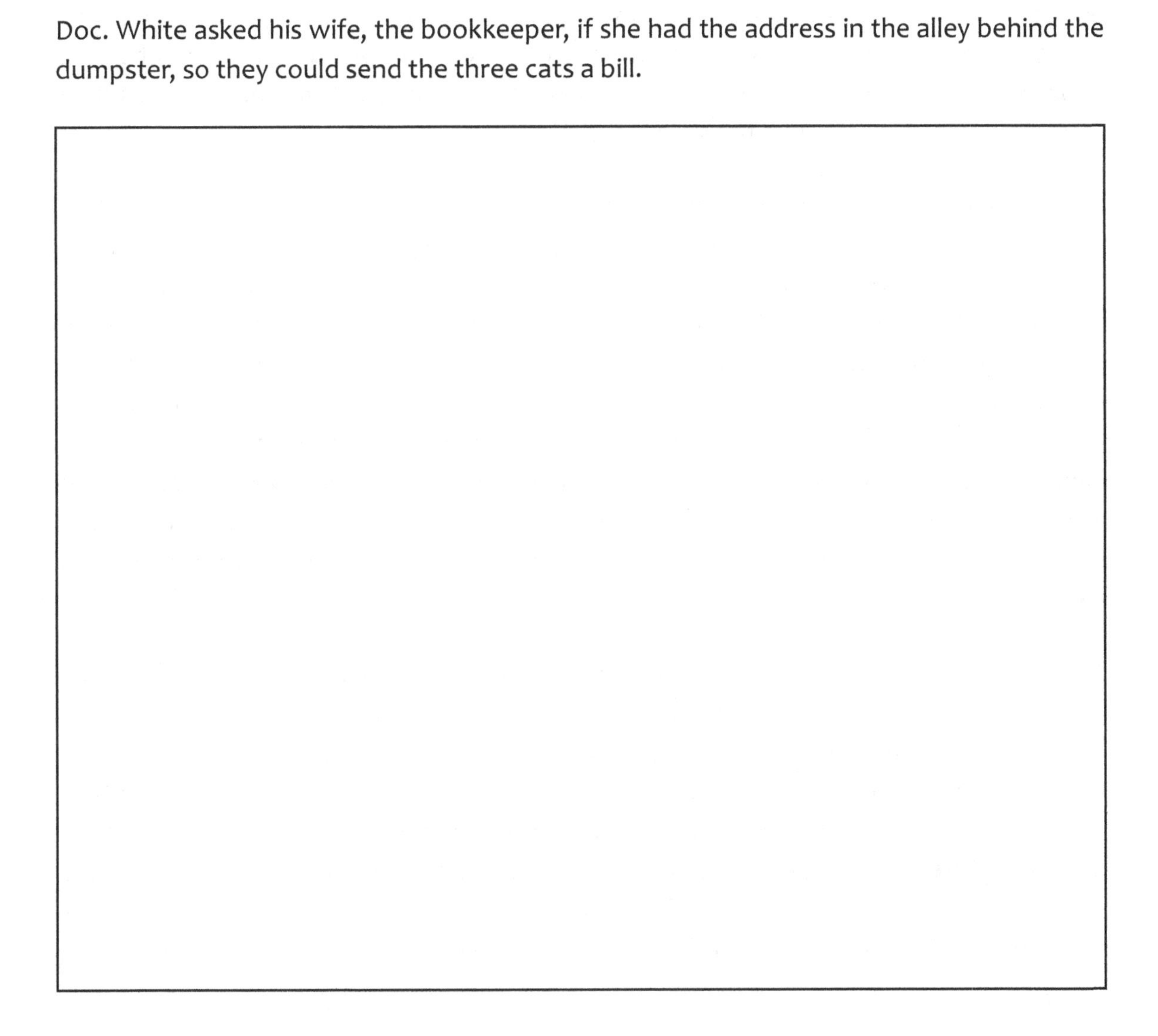

Can you sketch a bill or invoice for Dr. White to send to Yellowcat and his pals?

THREE CATS AND THE SOFT SPOT

In the hot summertime, the streets in Centerville tend to get a little soft, as the paving material reacts to the higher temperatures, and the asphalt becomes more pliable. The three cats, Alleycat, Tomcat, and Yellowcat, notice this and in the hottest time of the afternoon, on cloudless days, they know to be super careful where they put their feet. Really hot asphalt can seriously burn their paws, and is nearly impossible to remove. Cats don't like to be out and around in the heat anyway, so they mostly do their running errands during the cooler hours in the summer months. One spring month, probably April, they noticed a soft spot on the pavement near the curb next to Dollard's Department Store. It was soft, even sticky, even in the cool of the day. This puzzled the three cats as they carefully avoided stepping on the spot in the street.

Early one morning, the three were downtown on their way to the Fulton Street Fish Market, when they noticed the soft spot was covered by a delivery truck belonging to Dollard's. The driver was working in the back of the truck with the rear tailgate door open, as he checked his load before starting to go make his city deliveries. When they checked more closely, they could see that fuel was dripping from a big fuel tank of the truck, onto the pavement in the center of the soft spot (cats are naturally nosy about things, and gasoline and diesel fuel dilute asphalt, making it soft and sticky). The three cats tried to get the delivery truckdriver's attention, hoping to be able to show where his fuel drip was causing a problem and a possible fire hazard. The driver was engrossed in his counting duties and his only reaction to the three cats' attention-getting antics was to scold them and tell them "Scat!"

The three left to continue their way to the fish pier, to see the fishing boats unloading their catch from the previous day and last night's work. One of their favorite fishing boats, the Betsy Ross was unloading, and the crew were in high spirits because they were loaded with a fine catch. They tossed small fish onto the dock for the three cats, and several other cats congregated for the occasion. When the three cats were stuffed to the limit, the crew gave them three plastic bags loaded with fish scraps. The three showed their pleasure by meowing and started home. When they came by Dollard's, they checked the pavement soft spot and sure enough it was soft and runny and smelled of fuel, but the delivery truck was gone.

The next morning the three cats weren't in the mood for more good fish, but they went to the street beside Dollard's, and sure enough, the truck was parked in the same spot while the driver and another store employee were checking the load. The three cats stayed out of the way and mostly out of sight. Wanting to get the driver's attention without getting scolded again, they did something they had planned last night. Alleycat and Tomcat went to the soft spot where the fuel was dripping and carefully dipped one front paw each into the black goo. While Yellowcat kept watch to let them know if the driver headed their way, they each hopped upon the truck front bumper, and with their loaded paw free, they worked their way upon the hood, to get to the windshield in front of the driver's seat. You may have seen where a cat has left paw prints on a car's windshield sometime. These paw prints here weren't in brown dirt – they were black as tar, and as hard to remove. The two artists jumped down and started cleaning their "brushes," as they all three waited to see the driver's reaction to their art work.

They didn't have a long wait, and the resulting explosive reaction of the driver was worth the wait! He had settled into his seat and was securing his safety belt before his eyes fastened on the big, black cat's paw prints. He roared words the three cats rarely heard and jerked open his door and tried to get out without removing his belt. This caused another string of bad words ending in #%&**#@ CATS!!!

Then the three cats showed themselves, and when the driver with blood in his eyes charged at them, they scurried under the truck, where he had to get on his knees, and his right hand landed in the gooey mess his leaking fuel tank had caused. Seeing he had found the mess, the three cats cheerfully ran from under the truck and scampered home. The next week they saw the fuel leak had been fixed, and the soft spot on the street was almost back to normal. This made the three cats very happy.

Can you draw a few cat's paw prints using black pencil or crayon?

THREE CATS GO VISITING

The three cats were visiting Fluffy, Mrs. Pennyrich's Persian cat, in the backyard of the mansion on Sterling Street. They were allowed to do this since Mrs. Pennyrich liked them, because they have such good manners (at least for cats) and are nice to one another and to Fluffy. When the butler, Alfred, brought them kitty snacks, Mrs. Pennyrich was telling Alfred that she was planning on taking Fluffy with her next week when she and a friend were going to Havenwood Retirement Village to visit shut-ins. One nice elderly lady had seen a picture of Fluffy last month and said how she would like to see the real cat someday.

As she watched the four cats eating peacefully together, she mused about taking all four to the nursing home. When she mentioned this to Alfred, he rolled his eyes and asked if she was joking. This caused her to decide to do it.

Next week Alfred arrived in the alley where the three cats live and was lucky enough to find them there. He opened the door to the limo and Fluffy jumped to the ground as Alfred set down a big bowl of kitty snacks. While everyone enjoyed themselves with the food, he picked up the bowl and set it on the floor of the back seat area. All four cats jumped up into the limo, and Alfred gently closed the door and went around to the driver's seat and started the engine.

This didn't concern Fluffy in the least, but Tomcat, Alleycat and Yellowcat were somewhat alarmed. Seeing this, Alfred reached back and stroked them and spoke soothingly to them. With this assurance, and seeing Fluffy scarfing down "their" kitty snacks, they hardly noticed when the big car smoothly started out of the alley and turned toward its garage.

Mrs. Pennyrich and her church friend, Mrs. Hazalott, were glad to see the three friends of Fluffy in the limo and talked soothingly to them and petted them. All cats like to be petted when they are in relaxed mode. This may be true of lions and tigers ..., but they aren't in relaxed mode around humans very much. It took quite a lot of encouragement from the two ladies on the trip to the nursing home, because most cats don't enjoy the movements of a vehicle in motion, even a big limousine. Dogs, on the other hand, mostly just love riding in vehicles; many like putting their head out an open window with their stupid tongues hanging out of their mouths. Cats aren't dogs.

When they arrived at the nursing home, the lady in charge had some reservations about four unleashed felines running around inside, but allowed them in the open courtyard where a number of the residents were enjoying the nice day. Fluffy had been here before, and began to strut around to everyone's approval. One elderly resident, Mrs. Meeker, saw Tomcat and was reminded of her pet cat of years ago. She called Tomcat "General Ike" and was quite happy when Tomcat came to her and allowed her to rub his head. An old retired military man, Colonel Hawk, thought Alleycat resembled his old cat he had while stationed in France, and called him "Major" and offered him some leftover hot dog wiener. Alleycat/ Major eats almost anything, but really likes hot dog franks. He finished off the tasty morsel and curled up at the colonel's feet. Yellowcat found a rubber ball the nurses have for those patients who need to help their weakened grip, laying in a corner. He got it rolling and started swatting it with his forepaws, controlling which direction it rolled. Several of the people watched this and started laughing and encouraging him. Everyone in the courtyard had a happy time with the visiting group of cats, and the cats, all four, just loved the people and the attention. One little lady, Mrs. Weeker, saw all this from her room to which she was confined with a gout attack. She liked the appearance of Yellowcat and asked if she could have him brought in for a time. The administrator lady, seeing how well behaved the cats were being, okayed it, and Mrs. Pennyrich brought Yellowcat into the small room. He felt welcomed and loved by the tiny lady and laid down beside her bed and let her stroke his yellow brindle fur.

When it was time to go, Alfred picked up Fluffy and started toward the limo, and the three cats followed. The residents all started clapping and saying goodbye, asking when the cats might return.

Even Alfred had to admit the day had been very good as they started home.

THREE CATS VISIT TWO

When Mrs. Pennyrich planned another visit to Havenwood Retirement Village, she wanted to take her Persian cat, Fluffy. She recalled how well the three cats behaved last month and how everyone enjoyed them. With these things in mind, she asked Alfred if he could arrange getting the three cats ready to come too. Alfred got Fluffy in the limo and went to the three cats' alley, but they weren't home. He just drove out of the alley and parked under the shade of a big elm tree, where he could see down the alley where the three cats' cardboard box/home was in view behind the dumpster. Alfred was reading the newspaper, when Officer Dedmon stopped in his patrol car and asked if everything was okay. Alfred assured the policeman that everything was fine. He thought the reason he was sitting there would be hard to explain, so he just smiled as he assured the officer that he didn't need any help. Officer Dedmon returned the smile and said, "I guess you're waiting on the three cats so they can go with Mrs. Pennyrich and that cat of hers to the nursing home again this afternoon." Seems as if last month's visit had made news around town.

The three cats arrived home soon thereafter, just as Alfred was finishing with the sports page. When he drove the vehicle into the alley and stopped and opened the rear door, the three cats watched, and when they saw Fluffy they came closer. When Fluffy greeted them they responded by each one jumping up into the limo. Alfred closed the door with the same flourish as if three movie stars had just gotten into the car. As they were coming out onto the street, Mrs. Pennyrich rang his cell phone and Alfred told her he was headed home with all four cats.

When they arrived at the nursing home, there was no concern by the staff about the cats, since last time everything went so well. No one was thinking of the fact that Mr. Green, one of the residents, had his pet terrier, Pug, visiting him today. When the cats came into the courtyard, Pug was sleeping on the lounge chair next to Mr. Green who was reading a book. When one of the cats made a meow at another cat, Pug's ears went up, his eyes flew open, and he let loose a loud yap. The four cats hardly noticed, but continued their visiting with people and exploring around, pretty well ignoring Pug as they enjoyed everything. Several staff members were worried that there could be a problem and discussed what to do. Mr. Green simply talked soothingly to Pug and called to Yellowcat, who had been very friendly with him last month. Yellowcat came slowly toward Mr. Green and Pug, while holding his tail up with the tip curled down. He came and turned himself sidewise and began to rub his back on Mr. Green's feet which were extended over the end of the lounge chair.

Pug took Yellowcat's actions as being friendly and lowered his muzzle between his paws and watched the cat with interest. When Mr. Green placed his right hand on Pug's head and talked to him, he patted the chair cushion with his left hand and encouraged Yellowcat to come up onto the cushion. Yellowcat put his forepaws up there and watched to see what Pug would do. When Pug was still and quiet, Yellowcat slowly pulled himself up to the top and stretched out. When Pug wagged his tail and touched his nose to Yellowcat's nose, the people let out their breaths and some quietly clapped and started talking about how things had worked out. Mr. Green bragged on both Pug and Yellowcat and the ice was completely broken ..., and thawed. Before long, Pug was playing little games with all four of the feline visitors.

Each of the three cats, Tomcat, Alleycat, and Yellowcat, revisited with the people they saw last time, and made some new friends too. The manager, Miss Primms, and all the staff were happy that Mrs. Pennyrich and Mrs. Hazalott and Alfred had gone to the trouble to bring the four cats again to visit with and entertain them. While they were congratulating the cats, they also recognized Mr. Green and his dog, Pug, for turning a potential problem into a good example of animals putting aside old differences as treating one another in the way they wanted to be treated. This was a good example of the Golden Rule being applied by animals, who had never read or heard of that rule given by Jesus to His disciples. When it was time to go, Mrs. Pennyrich was already planning next month's visit with the nice people at Havenwood Retirement Village.

THREE CATS - MISS PRIMMS

Miss Primms was having thoughts of how to deal with a looming dilemma; how to best serve the people she was responsible for, while obeying the rules of the home office, without endangering her position at Havenwood Retirement Village. She dearly loved the residents – every one of them, even the ones who tried to be unlovable. She was very familiar with the rules of the home office, and how the headquarters staff enforced those rules. She liked her job as administrator of their premier Centerville operations. This job and these residents represented to her a continuation of her life's work. She had assumed the responsibilities of mother and father with her six siblings, when a tragic accident took their parents away from them, when she was still a teenager. Even though the state gave the kids foster parents, she was the authority figure to her brothers and sisters, After the youngest one finished college and got married, Miss Primms (Candy to her friends) started working at Havenwood as an orderly while she completed her college degree work.

Candy's present dilemma concerned the coming fall and winter season and the company rule against unleashed and multiple pets brought into the facility by visitors. She had bent the rules a little in allowing Mrs. Pennyrich to bring four cats, by stipulating they remain in the courtyard. Soon it would not be workable to do this as the courtyard would have no residents spending time there due to the cold weather. She desperately wanted to see the people enjoy the three cats and Fluffy, and she wanted Mrs. Pennyrich and Mrs. Hazalott to remain happy too. Mrs. Pennyrich was the residents' most loved person and most faithful visitor. She and Mrs. Hazalott funded the birdbath and fountain construction in the courtyard, as well as many other even more worthwhile projects and programs over the years. She had just recently discovered that the three cats were favorite pets of some kind at city hall – the city hall she had tussled with in recent years over a couple of questions regarding zoning matters.

If she elected to simply move things inside when cooler weather came, it might go unnoticed at headquarters, but a few animal foes might get the word delivered. Then it would become much more of a problem, and two of the directors favored others to fill her slot at Havenwood. If she had to tell Mrs. Pennyrich the cats' visits would have to be stopped until next summer, it might upset her and Mrs. Hazalott, and would make resuming things later a likely problem, since the courtyard excuse was already pretty thin. Even the assistant fire marshal recently commented on how his mother-in-law enjoyed the four cat's visits. He is the same nice fire marshal who was bugging her to update the fire alarm system in the old wing, where his mother-in-law is a resident. Candy rolled these conflicting things around in her head and thought of how much easier things would be for her if those three cats had stayed in their box/home she had heard about, but she realized she was only thinking of what would make her job easier, and not what was best for her people. She thought she could put the puzzle of what to do to Tom Steele, the nice lawyer, who helped her deal with city hall last year. He had asked her to lunch recently, and she had politely demurred due to end-of-the month paperwork that had piled up while her assistant was off on maternity leave.

She hesitated to renew her association with Tom, since he was obviously looking for a wife, and she had her family as they were growing up, and her present family consisting of the residents at Havenwood. She did have a set of problems that she felt unable to cope with, and she remembered that wise counsel is recommended in the Bible in the book of Proverbs and elsewhere. She read the ones in Proverbs 12:15 and 15:22, and decided to call Tom tomorrow.

Meanwhile, the three cats, Tomcat, Alleycat, and Yellowcat, were enjoying life and looking forward to the next time Alfred would arrive in their alley in the limo with Fluffy, to take them all to visit their many good friends at Havenwood. Any problems Miss Primms might have, that were caused by them weren't even on their radar.

THREE CATS AND THE TRAFFIC ACCIDENT

The three cats, Alleycat, Tomcat, and Yellowcat, were returning home late one summer afternoon from a nice visit down at the creek behind the big church building. As they got into the downtown area, they noticed the traffic was light on the streets. This made it easier for them to cross the necessary streets in relative safety. As they were almost safely across the last busy street, a big dump truck swerved to miss a car that had suddenly stopped in the middle traffic lane. Yellowcat and Tomcat had already gotten to the safety of the curb, but Alleycat was a little behind and was prevented from gaining the safety of the curb by some debris falling from the front of the still-moving truck. He spun quickly to get away when the massive front bumper and front fender almost hit him, and then the truck prevented the other cats from seeing where he was. There was lots of dust and dirt flying everywhere, and a crowd of people were gathering when someone yelled, "FIRE," as dense black smoke billowed from the rear part of the truck.

As the crowd stepped back quickly from the fire and smoke, the two cats jumped even more quickly to the branches of a tree, away from the threat of being trampled on. They hoped to get a glimpse of Alleycat from their elevated vantage point, but there were too many people and cars. Soon the fire department units arrived, along with the police. The fire was quickly suppressed, and traffic flow was reestablished by use of a detour route. Still no sign of Alleycat. Tomcat had the lower perch, so it was decided he would go home to see if Alleycat had made his way back. Yellowcat stayed where he could see if Alleycat was to be seen there.

Soon Yellowcat returned to tell Tomcat the sad news that Alleycat wasn't home, so they kept watching the scene of the accident. They overheard the police and fire officials saying that the truck driver was slightly hurt by striking his steering wheel, and that nobody else was hurt. Nothing was said about any cats or other animals.

As Tomcat and Yellowcat watched, the wrecker came and got the wrecked truck, and the wrecker driver helped the firefighters clean up the scene of broken glass and other debris. The firefighters hosed down the street, and the traffic safety cones were gathered and placed in the storage bin of one of the firetrucks. Everything returned to normal for everyone – everyone except two lonely, heartbroken cats who wearily climbed down and slowly started home to a vacant box behind a dumpster.

Neither cat had any appetite, so they didn't even eat the juicy meat Alleycat had earlier found "abandoned" in a backyard, while the barbecue cook and his guests were inside watching a tiebreaking field goal attempt on television. When the two lonely cats remembered how proud Alleycat had been of himself, they got big knots in their throats. They tried to get some sleep, but couldn't get comfortable. Every time they heard anything, they both ran outside hoping Alleycat was coming down the alley. Before midnight they went back to the scene, where they last saw their buddy racing from the runaway truck. It was eerily quiet as very few vehicles were moving on the street. There was no evidence there had been an accident and fire there recently. They had earlier seen no blood or hair on the street, and there was none now. Their hearts ached as they tried to be brave and think Alleycat was okay somewhere now. They reluctantly returned home and got very little fitful sleep as they missed their buddy.

Early the next morning they returned to the scene, but saw nothing except the usual rush hour traffic and heard an occasional beep of a horn. This was the loneliest-busiest place imaginable for Yellowcat and Tomcat. They returned home, and although neither of them felt really hungry, they felt it would be unappreciative on their part to let Alleycat's last food effort go to waste, so they nibbled at the good food.

In the days to come, the two remaining cats were heartbroken and sad as they mourned the loss of their almost lifetime companion. They were unusually considerate of one another and rarely left their box/home for anything, as if not wanting to be gone if their pal should by some miracle return.

RETURN OF ALLEYCAT

Alleycat awakened in strange surroundings – in someone's house inside a baby's bed, surrounded by dolls and toys. Alleycat was confused and aching all over; and it hurt every time he took a breath. He could hear several people talking, including some children, but no one was in the dimly lit room where he was. At first Alleycat couldn't remember anything much of recent events, but he had a dim recall of lots of people, and noise, and thick, black smoke. As he tried to recall more, he then recalled something hard had hit his head and then nothing until he woke up here in this strange house in a child's bed. He was really thirsty, and it hurt to move anything. Soon two kids came into the room and looked at him. The girl spun around, ran into the hallway and shouted, "Hey, the cat's awake!"

The family members were all good to Alleycat – they were all happy he was awake, and the mother told the kids they might offer him some water. The water was very good, if a mite too cold, and Alleycat lapped it up with relish, even though his throat hurt when he swallowed. Later they brought him some chicken and gravy. He slowly ate most of the good tasting gravy and nibbled at the meat, but his throat hurt when he tried to get the meat down. The whole family came in after dinner and looked at him and marveled that he was still alive. The man looked at Alleycat's tag and said he would call the telephone number tomorrow. Alleycat felt a little better and was glad to see they had placed a sand box near his bed. He slept fitfully that night, wondering if Tomcat and Yellowcat were doing okay and if they were home or not.

The next morning Alleycat awakened early, before the family was stirring, and realized his throat felt better, and it hardly hurt at all when he breathed. When the mother started cooking breakfast in the kitchen, he realized how hungry he was, as the aroma of frying bacon and eggs wafted into his room. Alleycat was a little timid about barging into the kitchen, but he overcame his shyness and ventured out into the hall. Walking hurt some, but not like yesterday, and Alleycat followed his nose to where those good smells were coming from. When he entered the kitchen, the lady cooking only looked down at him and said, "Well good morning mister cat – aren't we looking better this morning." Then she added, "I bet you're hungry now." With that she set a bowl of scrambled eggs on the floor and then some water too. The water was good ..., but the eggs were even better.

When the man called the number on Alleycat's tag, the dispatcher at City Fire Station #3 answered and was elated that the caller said he had a cat he had retrieved a couple of days ago at an accident scene downtown. Ten minutes later the assistant fire chief and two others arrived in the chief's official car and thanked the Collins family for taking such good care of Alleycat and for calling them. When they departed, Mr. Collins told the family that evidently that cat belonged to some of the brass at the fire department judging by the way they had responded. The family was all in agreement, because the cat was well-behaved and friendly, although he looked like just an ordinary alley cat.

Back at the box/home in the alley behind the garbage dumpster, Yellowcat and Tomcat were moping around and feeling sad because they had given up most of their earlier hope that Alleycat was somehow safe, somewhere, somehow. When the fire department vehicle turned into the alley, they hardly noticed. When it stopped, they were slightly interested. When the rear door opened, they saw a fireman getting out, so they watched. When he turned around with Alleycat in his arms, they went crazy. The two cats mobbed the fireman in getting to Alleycat, who was as happy as they were, but unable to be as active in showing it as they were, because he was still somewhat stiff and weak feeling.

The three cats were very happy to be reunited, and Alleycat's story was eagerly listened to by the other two. His picture was in the paper with some of the fire station's crew, and then the incident was pretty well forgotten except by the three cats, the fire department people, and the Collins family, who said they wanted to visit the three cats someday.

THREE CATS EARLY DAYS

There have been some folks, whom have inquired regarding why the three cats, Tomcat, Yellowcat, and Alleycat, do not have a normal home like most cats. We thought that was a good question, so we asked the three cats to walk down memory lane or maybe we should say memory alley, and share with us what they remember. We've discussed before; how cats have very good memories.

Tomcat remembers his life began like most little kittens. He was one of several siblings. He also had a mother cat who loved all her little kittens and provided for their every need. They lived in a nice backyard that belonged to a dad, a mom, and two young children. Tomcat always felt loved in his home and enjoyed scampering, playing, and climbing with his sibling kittens in the big tall trees.

Tomcat thought it would be this way forever, but things began to change. One by one, his brother and sister kittens left, and he never saw them again. Although he was lonely and missed them, he felt that he would always have his mother cat. However, he remembers one day she was taken to the vet because she wasn't feeling well, and she never came home again. Then the mom and dad, and both the little children were especially attentive to Tomcat. They must have sensed that he would be scared and lonely without his cat family.

Things went well for a while, but one day Tomcat saw a huge moving van, and the family and the workers were loading all the furniture into the van. Tomcat didn't want to be a part of that, so he hid behind some thick bushes in the backyard and didn't come out when they called him. Soon however, Tomcat was alone with no human family to care for him. He began to look for ways to find food and became a pal to a nice friendly cat called Yellowcat. Yellowcat showed him all the tricks of the trade and how to look in all the right places to find his favorlte foods. As they swapped stories, they learned a lot about each other. At one time Yellowcat also had a mother cat and some siblings. Yellowcat remembers leaving his cat family and going to live with a gentle, older man who showed much love to Yellowcat.

This new home with the "Pastor," as he was called by his friends, was a happy time for Yellowcat. The Pastor named him "Sunshine." He explained to his group of friends that after he lost his lifelong friend, his beloved wife, that his cat had put sunshine back into his life. Sunshine was allowed to listen in and to be a part of what the Pastor and his friends called "Bible Study." There were always many little children there, which made Sunshine feel more comfortable, because they were gentle with him and enjoyed seeing and playing with Sunshine. All that was required of Sunshine and the little children was to sit quietly and listen as they discussed these important matters.

Sunshine learned that the human family looks forward to a better life in a place called Heaven. This is a place that has been prepared by the Creator God called "Jesus" for His children. Once Sunshine heard one of the grownups say, "God even knows when a little sparrow falls to the ground."

This was especially interesting and comforting for Sunshine to hear. In the days to come, he would share these important things with Tomcat and Alleycat, so they also could be comforted. Sunshine's life was easy with the Pastor, but one day Sunshine saw an ambulance come to their home to take the Pastor away. Sunshine never saw the Pastor again.

Tomcat listened as Yellowcat related all these things to him. Sunshine's name had been changed to Yellowcat after he became a member of the alley cat community. Tomcat was so happy he had been able to meet Yellowcat, and now they had become best buddies, as they made their home in the cardboard box behind the dumpster in the alley between Elm & Cherry Avenues.

The alley cats all over town were beginning to be concerned regarding their safety. Word had spread quickly that a new animal control officer had been hired by the city, and he was doing a great job in helping control the stray cats and dogs in the community. Tomcat and Yellowcat took turns being on lookout for the pickup truck. It is a well-known fact around the alley cat world that a new animal control officer does a great job, until he becomes friendly with some of the strays. This always hinders his job performance somewhat, and then the stray cats are able to relax a little.

Tomcat and Yellowcat had been dumpster diving in their dumpster in front of their cardboard box/home along with another cat called Alleycat, when Yellowcat alerted the others that the pickup truck had just now turned into the alley off Elm Avenue. When the two made a jump into their home, Alleycat was caught off-guard and wasn't sure where to go. Yellowcat said, "Hurry, come into our home with us, you'll be safe here." With one quick leap, Alleycat was visiting in the home of his newly found friends. The pickup truck continued down the alley and turned onto Cherry Avenue. The three cats each took a deep breath and began to relax. After they discussed their close call, Alleycat almost felt at home with the others. The two cats shared with Alleycat all about themselves, and wanted to know all about Alleycat. Alleycat told them all he could remember about his past.

Tomcat and Yellowcat had experienced a taste of the finer things in life. Not so with Alleycat. It seemed it was always a struggle for Alleycat to have enough to eat. He remembers his mother cat, who loved him and always tried to bring him enough food. He acquired a taste for anything and everything that could be found by his mother cat. He remembers his mother would spend hours combing his coat with her tongue to keep his hair beautiful, smooth, & clean. Alleycat felt safe with his mother cat, and she taught him to never trust a member of the human family. He remembered that lesson well, and to this day he preferred to have no contact with them, although he has learned from his pals that many of them are kind and to be trusted. Alleycat never knew what happened to his mother cat. She left one day to find food for them and she never returned.

Alleycat was on his own and he tried to live by the law of the alley cat world. He once found himself in the middle of a cat and dog fight, where he lost a chunk from his right ear. Anyway, he learned an important lesson; never try to be pals with bad, bully cats! Alleycat was so happy when Tomcat and Yellowcat invited him to join them in their box/home and be a part of their team.

In recent times the three cats have attained some measure of fame in Centerville. But they are still content with whom they are; just three cats living behind the dumpster in the alley between Elm and Cherry Avenues. They love the freedom to run and play all over their city, enjoy seeing all the familiar sights that they know so well, and investigating anything that is new. Inside their alley cat world they want to encourage their brothers and sisters to love and help one another, not to be bullies, and to make life more pleasant for their human friends.

Someone once said, "A dragon lives forever." So it may be that the three cats may live for many years in the hearts and minds of a few grandpas and grandmas, and some moms and dads, and hopefully many little children. We all enjoy being in a safe place. Probably there is no safer place for the three cats to be.

THREE CATS AND THE LINEMAN

The three cats noticed the boom truck drive slowly down their alley, as the driver peered at the telephone and power wires overhead. They had seen this before from time to time. Then the truck stopped at a utility pole that supported several power lines and some telephone cables and wires. The three cats were paying more attention to things now. Cats are curious by nature, and they watch closely whenever something different is happening.

The man got out of the truck and carefully noted where it was positioned in reference to the cables and wires overhead. He then deployed the out-rigger supports which give the boom truck good support when the boom is extended. The lineman got into the big, white, fiberglass bucket and using the remote control, raised himself up, where he could more closely examine the cables and wires. He was moving some of the wires with his gloved hand, and when he pulled his hand back the glove dropped into the bucket. He put his bare hand back into the wires and jerked back quickly while making a loud sound. He then slumped down with his head and arms outside of the bucket. At that time his handheld radio fell from his jacket pocket to the ground.

The three cats instinctively realized the man was in trouble and ran to the radio, since the slick pole was not possible to climb, to get themselves to the man. Tomcat had seen the police and fire people use their radios enough to know the small button or lever on the side of the device must be pressed in order to talk on it. He found the push-button on the lineman's radio and pressed it with his paw. The little red light came on, and when he released it a woman's voice came from the speaker saying, "Go ahead unit thirty-six - - - this is base, unit thirty-six over." Tomcat pressed the button again and meowed into the microphone and released the button. The dispatcher lady tried again to establish contact with the unit whose call number was displayed on her control console. No answer but the meowing of a cat.

The dispatcher then called a supervisor's radio and reported the unusual things that were going on. The supervisor agreed with the dispatcher that it was probably nothing to be too concerned about, but asked her for the GPS coordinates displayed for the radio of unit thirty-six. With this information he quickly arrived at the location and discovered the unconscious lineman up in his cherry-picker unit. The fire department was called and another boom truck was summoned. The EMT persons got the lineman down and transported to the hospital. The utility people were still in the alley examining the work area to determine what had caused the lineman to be hurt, when word came over the radio saying the lineman was doing okay at the emergency room, and the doctors were going to keep him there at the hospital overnight to make sure he had no permanent damage.

The camera crew from Action Nine News was there in the alley and arranged with the utility supervisor to have the handheld radio placed on the ground with the boom truck in the background and the three cats posing with the radio between them. Of course, this led to the newspaper reporters and camera crew coming to the alley and getting a few shots of the three cats to run in the newspaper. The fire chief became involved also, when the news organizations sought him out, along with the utility company's dispatcher and local manager. When the lineman was released from the hospital these photo ops were all restaged until the three cats became tired of it all, and went to the creek behind the big church to do some quiet fishing. The three cats agreed among themselves that they hoped the news hounds never discovered their fishing hole location.

The problem with the wires and cables was corrected and things returned to normal in the alley between Cherry and Elm Avenues. The cardboard box/home of the three cats, located behind the trash dumpster returned to its normal quiet state and the three cats returned to their mundane lives and hoped the next time the utility company's cherry-picker truck came down their alley, it would keep going to find trouble and excitement somewhere else.

THREE CATS AND THE LOOT

Sometimes it's not so much what we hear or see, as much as the time we hear or see it. It was sometime after midnight, that the three cats heard running footsteps in the alley where they live. Then the footsteps stopped, and something thumped against the fence behind their cardboard box/home. They felt it bounce against the box. The footsteps continued down the alley more slowly, and were soon out of hearing range. Cats have very good hearing, which serves them well in staying safe and in finding food. White cats with blue eyes often have less acute hearing, especially as they get older. None of the three cats fit this description.

Next morning the cats looked behind their box/home and found a money bag stuffed full of big denomination bills. The money bag had the name of one of the big stores downtown on it. While Yellowcat stayed there to safeguard the money, Tomcat and Alleycat went to the police station to get Sergeant O'Malley to send someone with them. They went straight to his little office, but the good officer was busy with some papers. Knowing the cats wanted something based on their actions, he told the dispatcher to call the nearest patrol car to go with the cats to see what they had a bee in their bonnets about.

Hearing this, Tomcat and Alleycat sped outside and started toward home. The dispatcher, seeing this, and knowing some of the antics of the past with the cats, simply called the patrol unit and directed it to meet the cats in their alley. When the two cats arrived home, the police unit was already there, and the two officers were talking to Yellowcat. Alleycat wasted no time in showing the two young officers the money bag. The officers were excited and called for a detective unit to come to where they were.

The two plainclothes detectives arrived in an unmarked police unit and were also excited about the find and bragged on the three cats for alerting the authorities. The three watched as the men carefully placed the money bag inside a large evidence envelope, shot a few camera pictures, and left as quickly as they came. A few hours later they returned with the money bag and carefully placed it where it had been. After they got it positioned just where they wanted, one pulled a long cord from the bag and announced, "Okay, the dye charge is set." The other one turned to the attentive cats and told them they should leave it alone. As they were leaving, they were laughing about how the three cats would look in bright, Dayglo orange if they messed with the money bag.

The three cats actually understood more of what had been said to them than either detective even supposed. They stayed away from the bag as much as possible, considering that it was wedged between their box and the alley fence. They had heard enough "shop talk" to know the police had found fingerprints on the bag, so they were looking for a perp named Henry, the Heister. The next day just before sunset, a strange car drove through the alley and slowed somewhat, as it passed by the dumpster in front of the three cats' home. The car sped up a bit as it left the alley, and an unmarked police car pulled away from the curb a block behind it. Ten minutes later the car entered the alley from the other end, placing the passenger's side nearest the dumpster, and stopped. A small fat man jumped out and ran behind the dumpster for only a few seconds, returning with the money bag, gleefully saying to the driver that the bag was still there and he had it in his hands. The car started toward the exit, but a marked police unit blocked their escape.

The driver of the bad car started backing up fast, only to see the unmarked police unit block that end too. Policemen were out of both cars and with their guns drawn were telling the crooks that they were under arrest. The driver put his hands up, but the guy with the bag quickly jumped out and started to try to climb the alley fence. He was too short and fat to make it easily, and the policemen were converging on him when the timed-release dye charge exploded in a great cloud of brilliant Dayglo orange dye. Henry the Heister stumbled from the cloud looking like he was already wearing an orange jail jumpsuit. The three cats avoided that orange spot in their alley for the next few weeks.

Draw a moneybag with drawstrings. You can decide the store name.

THREE CATS VISIT THE MOTHER HEN

The three cats were reminded of their earlier experience, when the brown chicken hen escaped from a dropped cage, when she took refuge in their cardboard box/home. She had hatched some eggs there, and they had been able to get her and her chicks taken to a farm near the city. Whenever they saw chickens, this happy interlude in their lives was recalled. They wanted to visit the mother hen and her family of chicks to see how they were doing. They knew the kindly farmer who took the chickens to his place, also brought eggs and vegetables to the farmer's market on a regular basis. With all these things in mind, the three visited the farmer's market and sought the particular man they were looking for. Sure enough, they found him and his wife and a daughter at their booth. They had eggs, butter, cheese, and tomatoes displayed for sale. As soon as the farmer espied the three cats, he was happy and told his wife and daughter that these cats were the ones he had told them about when he brought "Buffy" and her chicks home recently.

Of course, stray animals aren't allowed to roam around at the farmer's market ..., but the three cats are hardly stray cats in Centerville. With their special status in the town, the three cats are likely to be seen and accepted almost anywhere. They made themselves at home at the farmer's booth and were the reason several people came by to see the famous felines. The farmer's daughter was fascinated with the three as the passerbys recounted some of their better known exploits for public service. She picked Tomcat up and stroked his fur and hugged him. She put some milk in a bowl and set it in a shady spot for the three. She took a damp cloth and cleaned most of the mustard and catsup from Alleycat's coat, and exclaimed to her parents about his pretty calico coloring. This all caused Yellowcat to feel somewhat neglected, so he purposely rubbed himself against her ankle, meowed and looked plaintively up to her. The girl giggled, picked him up, mussed his fur around his ears and called him her mini-tiger.

When the farmer and the ladies closed up shop early, his wife commented on how the good crowd they had because of the cats, helped them to sell out early. They weren't surprised when the three cats made themselves welcome and jumped up in the bed of the pickup. They weren't just not surprised, they insisted the three ride in the cab with them. The ride to the farm wasn't very far, and they arrived before midafternoon. The three cats went out into the backyard and soon the farmer brought Buffy and her chicks there. To refer to them as chicks is a stretch ..., they were all handsome chickens, every one of them the exact rich brown color of their mother. The mother hen, recalling the many kindnesses of the three cats, cluck-clucked her warm regard for them and was completely at ease. Her brood, on the other hand, were somewhat restrained toward the cats ..., after all they are cats.

The ladies brought some food in a bowl and set it and some water down for the cats, and some grain in another bowl, which they scattered on the ground. The cats and chickens became busy eating their respective foods in their respective manners. The cats lapping, and the chickens pecking. The farmer took a few snapshots to commemorate the unusual occurrence. His wife commented that this event reminded her of the Scripture in the Bible at Isaiah 11:6-7, where it says, *The wolf also shall dwell with the lamb, and the leopard shall lie down with the kid; and the calf and the young lion and the fatling together; and a little child shall lead them. And the cow and the bear shall feed; their young ones shall lie down together; and the lion shall eat straw like the ox.* This prophetic passage refers to the perfect kingdom after Jesus returns. When you read this Scripture, take time to read all of chapter eleven, it speaks of a wonderful period of peace. It also mentions Egypt, Syria and countries appearing in today's news dispatches.

The three cats enjoyed their visit and spent the night there with the farmer's family and Buffy and hers. The next day the farmer, wife and daughter returned the three cats to where he had met them earlier – their cardboard box/home in the alley between Cherry and Elm. The three cats now had another interesting memory to recall in the future. So did the farmer and his family and Buffy and hers.

Try drawing a hen and seven chicks, like the sketch Cameron left here.

THREE CATS - MISS PRIMMS - AND THE BOARD

Miss Primms, the administrator of Havenwood Retirement Village called the attorney, Tom Steele, who had been so helpful with dealing with the city council last year, and they met for lunch. She explained the dilemma created by the rule forbidding unleashed and multiple pets brought into the facility by visitors. She told Tom how much the residents enjoyed the visits by the three cats and Fluffy, when Mrs. Pennyrich and Mrs. Hazalott bring them. Tom already knew of the importance of keeping those two ladies happy. Tom, the lawyer, said he needed a little time to consider these matters. Tom, the suitor, suggested a dinner meeting Friday evening, after business hours.

Friday evening Tom picked Candy up at her apartment and they drove to The Shrimp Boat restaurant out on the cape. They enjoyed a relaxed meal and discussed things going on in their lives. They finally discussed the problems of wanting to get permission from the home office to allow the three cats and Fluffy to be brought into Havenwood as a group. Tom outlined to Candy his plan to have her appeal directly to the board of directors for the corporation, as their administrator – and as a stockholder of record with the company. Candy commented on how brilliantly simple this was and showed how pleased she was with Tom's strategy. Tom cautioned that they needed to hold off on the celebration until they saw how it all played out ...

The next week Tom arranged with a stockbroker friend to quietly acquire one hundred shares of the holding company that owned Havenwood, in Candy Primm's name. Candy, meanwhile, arranged to attend the upcoming stockholder's and director's meeting in Capitol City next month.

When time came to go to the meetings in Capitol City, the group included Candy and Tom with Mrs. Pennyrich and Mrs. Hazalott with Alfred in the limo, and the four cats with four of the residents who really loved the cats, in the Havenwood van, driven by resident, and retired General Hawk. When Candy spoke to the directors at the meeting, she told them how the people at Havenwood enjoyed and looked forward to the cats coming each time. She said they had gained three new residents because of the tales others had told about the cats' visits. When one of the directors Mr. Grumpi, challenged her for skirting the rules by having the cats' appearances in the courtyard, Candy allowed her attorney friend, Tom Steele to answer in her behalf. Tom respectfully explained that it had started as a one-time occasion, but the cats were so popular with the residents that it was continued. He further offered to have the four cats brought into the meeting, so the directors could observe for themselves what they were discussing. On a procedure vote the board unanimously approved the cats being brought in.

The cats in spite of feeling a little giddy from traveling were on their very best behavior, since they all sensed that this was an important occasion for Miss Primms and Tom Steele, whom they all liked. They all four walked around and visited with all the board members and the directors seemed to feel good toward their visitors. When they had made the rounds of visiting others, they came to where the other visitors were and curled up near Tom and Candy.

When Tom again addressed the board, he said he knew they had more important things to consider in tending to the corporation's business matters. When he was asked by Mr. Grumpi what he proposed to do if the board failed to approve a rules change to accommodate Miss Primms' position, Tom said they would await the vote on the administrator's request. He added that in the event the vote was negative, he was prepared to enter the considerations by representing the position of shareholder Primms before the ensuing stockholder's meeting.

This all wasn't to Mr. Grumpi's liking, but the rest of the board were amused at the clever maneuvering on Tom's part. The matter was presented as a motion at the proper time and passed easily on a voice vote to allow an exception to the visiting animals rule for Havenwood.

On the triumphant return to Havenwood everyone and the cats, except Tom and Candy rode in the van. Those two had the big limo to themselves with Alfred driving. The three cats somehow felt as if they had done something good for all the residents, and Tom and Candy (their good friends).

THREE CATS GET INSIDE

After Miss Candy Primms and Attorney Tom Steele stole the show with the three cats at the director's meeting, things returned to normal for the cats. They were brought to Havenwood Retirement Village by Mrs. Pennyrich, and Mrs. Hazalott, and the driver, Alfred. They visited the residents and staff out in the large, central courtyard just as in the past. Now, however they were free to visit individuals and groups inside. This made their monthly visits more enjoyable to many more people. Candy planned for the coming fall and winter weather in many ways, including the cats' visits.

After the first cold snap in the late fall, the three cats with Mrs. Pennyrich's cat, Fluffy, were brought into the main visiting room. This room, while large, wasn't as roomy as the courtyard, but lots warmer with the central heat and big fireplace. One of the older ladies, Mrs. Toler, was knitting near the side of the fireplace and had a large ball of yellow yarn in a basket near her wheelchair. When she vigorously jerked on the yarn to get it uncaught, the big yellow ball jumped out of the basket and rolled toward the fireplace hearth. Yellowcat, quick as a flash intercepted the rolling ball and expertly batted it back toward the basket. This action caught the attention of several residents who spontaneously started clapping and yelling "bravo" to Yellowcat. Seeing how everyone enjoyed all this, Mrs. Toler asked a staff member to get the yarn ball and hand it to her. She then cut the yarn and secured the loose end securely to the surface of the ball. Everyone was watching to see what she was going to do with the ball, when she called Yellowcat and rolled the yarn ball quickly toward him. Yellowcat caught on to what was expected of him, and raced to bunt the ball toward Alleycat, who batted the ball to Tomcat.

This continued as Fluffy stretched and jumped from a lady's lap to join in the game of pass the yarn, to everyone's delight. When lunchtime was announced in the dining room, some of the residents moved in that direction, and the four cats tired of the game and returned to visiting with individual residents. The kitchen staff prepared plates for the few residents, who were confined in their rooms, and Alfred helped one of the cooks fix bowls of savory food for Alleycat, Tomcat, Yellowcat, and Fluffy. Alfred then joined Mrs. Pennyrich, Mrs. Hazalott, and Candy at the head table. Candy asked Alfred to say a blessing for the meal, which he did just before Tom Steele hastily entered the room asking everyone's pardon for arriving late. No one seemed to realize he was late except himself and Candy, who pointed to the empty seat and plate and silverware next to her.

When someone at the table inquired why Tom came to lunch there that particular day, (although it was pretty apparent) Tom politely explained that since this was the first day all four cats were allowed inside, he just wanted to see everything go smoothly. A couple of the girls serving food exchanged glances, rolled their eyes and giggled a little at this. Everyone enjoyed their meal and afterward, the four cats divided up and visited the shut-ins in the various rooms, where the staff had left doors open and the head nurse, Miss Wells, supervised the various visits to those patients, who were well enough to enjoy a visit from a well-behaved, warm, and caring feline.

When time came to end their first inside visit, the cats and their human friends returned to their homes. Fluffy returned to his sequin-encrusted canopy bed and the three cats to their cardboard box/home behind the dumpster in the alley between Cherry and Elm downtown. The three cats really enjoyed going to the nursing home and seeing how the people there always seemed to get a lift in their spirits when the cats did just ordinary things like they did every day elsewhere. Fluffy and the two ladies and Alfred liked getting out and doing something for others. Candy Primms felt fulfilled when the residents were doing so well and having happy lives. She also appreciated the low turnover they were experiencing at Havenwood, and the warm praise they were getting from the home office. Attorney Tom Steele was relishing his free, "pro bono" work for the retirement facility and his arrangements developing with its administrator, Candy, whom he called Miss Primms.

THREE CATS OVERNIGHT AT THE MANSION

The three cats, Tomcat, Yellowcat, and Alleycat, were returning from a visit at Havenwood Retirement Village with their friend Fluffy and their human friends. As they were loading up into the big limo the driver, Alfred, noticed a big, black storm cloud approaching, so they all hurried getting into the vehicle and out of the fresh wind. Before they had gotten half way home the rain started and increased in intensity, so the wipers weren't able to keep the windshield clear of sheets of rainwater. When they arrived at Mrs. Pennyrich's big mansion it was nice to be able to pull into the garage and have the overhead door closed against the gale-driven rain. As they were getting out of the car, Mrs. Pennyrich asked Alfred to get the three cats out too, since the rainstorm was making driving unsafe.

Mrs. Hazalott called her driver and told him she was spending the night at the Pennyrich house, so he could pick her up tomorrow around nine. The three cats followed Fluffy into his room where fresh water and a bowl of kitty snacks were already there before the pantry maid brought their evening food; and what food it was! Small sardines in a creamy sauce, with small English tea biscuits. They got really stuffed on that, not knowing there was French vanilla ice cream coming too. The three cats were oohing and aahing about this, when Fluffy said the desert was better when the ice cream was softer, and served topping fresh flan the chef excelled in making.

After the supper dishes and bowls were whisked away the four cats watched television on Fluffy's set tuned to the pet channel. The evening's offering was showing a dog show in London, so they left that to play with Fluffy's automatic soap bubble-blowing gizmo. Whenever Fluffy wanted help with anything ..., or just wanted to show out, there was a big red button to be pressed, which rang a bell in the pantry area so the maid could come and attend to Fluffy's request. The maid couldn't understand cat language, but she was good at guessing what was wanted most of the time. At bedtime the cats each found a nice soft spot to his liking and curled up for a good night's sleep.

Next morning the maid brought the cats four bowls and poured warm milk into them, followed by soft, scrambled eggs just like the ladies were enjoying in the breakfast alcove next to the big kitchen.

The storm had passed after midnight, and except for some flooded areas in the city, traffic was running about normal. Alfred was needing to go to the hardware store for some supplies so he took the three cats home in the pickup truck. When he turned into their alley all three of the cats were standing on the seat peering to see what shape their box was in. This amused Alfred and he told them to take it easy, since their box fared well in last night's storm because the heavy plastic wrapping the firemen had put around the box had protected it well.

Alfred unloaded some dry cotton batting Mrs. Pennyrich sent and a half sack of kitty snacks before he left to go shopping. The three cats were glad to be back home, where they felt at ease among their own stuff. Alleycat stretched out on some of the new cotton in his corner and started looking around as if he was missing something. When Tomcat asked him what was the matter, he replied, "Where's that big red button to call for some cool seltzer-water and to get my pillow fluffed the way I like it?" They all laughed and agreed they had enjoyed seeing how Fluffy lived, but were happy to be back home in their simpler surroundings.

I guess we can all identify with the three cats here. We all enjoy traveling and visiting other people in their different surroundings, but it is always so good to get back home in familiar digs with our own family and friends. When we visit other cultures we learn things to use in our lives, and we usually see things elsewhere that make us even more thankful for the blessings we receive from our Maker and those we interact with.

That night there was no ice cream, with or without freshly made flan, but the three cats enjoyed sharing a good sized pizza crust from the dumpster behind Don Carleons' cafe, before turning in on their own beds.

Do you want to draw and color some pizza scraps? Use red and orange for slices of pepperoni and pesto and yellow and orange for cheese.

THREE CATS AND THE GRAND OPENING

The mayor of Centerville has a son, who is a decorated war hero whose name is Sam Bigger. Sam and a buddy named Mike Durant returned from overseas service with the U.S. Marines to the same veteran's hospital in Capitol City for rehab following field hospital surgery, caused by damage to their feet and lower legs when an enemy IED exploded. Sam and Mike decided to open an auto service center in downtown Centerville when they were discharged from rehab. They picked a location where an old abandoned shoe factory building was slowly crumbling apart. Mayor Jimmy Bigger encouraged their enterprise as being a good opportunity for them and a big help in restoring some business activity in the central part of the town.

As they were discussing their plans at the mayor's home one evening, Mike noticed a picture of the mayor with the three cats sitting on the piano in the living room. Mike asked about the cats and the mayor related how they had made the news several times in recent days, and had gotten their pictures in the newspaper. When Mike asked where the three cats lived, the mayor said it was somewhere around Fire Station #3 and close to where the proposed auto service center was being planned.

This led to Mike and Sam discussing the possibility of having the three cats featured at their grand opening, when the time came for that occasion. These plans were temporarily forgotten, as they returned to the many details of getting their vision off the ground. They had consulted another hometown veteran to help, a structural engineer and architect. He had helped in planning to use the existing foundation and concrete floor and upright beams to build their new building around. They planned for a system of allowing people employed in the shops and offices still located downtown to drop off their cars for oil changes, light mechanical work, washing, waxing, and detailing services. The work started soon after the mayor and a few of his business friends arranged the needed financing.

Of course, as soon as the first work began, the three cats noticed and were interested in what was happening. Cats always notice anything new or different in their world, and always are curious as to what is going on. When Mike and Sam visited the construction site the three cats were watching from a nearby shady bush. They, of course, immediately saw Mike's seeing-eye dog, Rusty, and could see that Mike depended on him to guide his walking around the uneven and changing walking area. When the mayor and police chief stopped by, the chief, always alert, espied the three cats sitting under the big bush. He mentioned this to the mayor who called Mike and Sam to see the now famous trio. When the mayor called for the three to come to him, Mike spoke quietly to Rusty, who promptly sat at ease beside his handler. The three cats had learned long ago not to judge everyone and everything, including dogs, based on stereotypes. They took Rusty's relaxed attitude to be a good sign and warily came to the mayor. This led to later meetings being on easy, friendly terms, as the three cats acted as if Rusty was a big, affable cat, instead of a dog.

In the final days of installing furnishings and equipment at the attractive new-on-the-outside building, the two service veterans were pondering what to name their venture. They finally decided to name it "Three Cats Service Center," since it had become a habit for the trio to be there almost every day anyway, and the citizens of Centerville had almost adopted them. Tom's wife, Mitzi, made cute little jackets for the three cats bearing the new company's logo, depicting three handsome cats in a circle of red, white and blue. It was a beautiful summer day when the grand opening was held. The featured items included a big barbecue and ice cream feast with a brass band from the fire department, a barbershop quartet including Mrs. Pennyrich's driver, Alfred, at bass. The local Marine Corp's marching paraders were there, and of course, the three cats. His Honor, Mayor Jimmy Bigger made a magnificent speech, which some in attendance felt was a mite too long. He touched on how important it was to the citizens that the downtown be used more and encouraging the people to live there instead of fleeing to the suburbs. He bragged on Sam and Mike a little, and on himself and his administration a lot. Then the mayor mentioned the three cats, and their new namesake business, which drew a loud round of applause, as His Honor headed toward the barbecue line.

THREE CATS AND THE TURTLE

The three cats, Alleycat, Tomcat, and Yellowcat, were in their box/home behind the dumpster in the alley between Cherry and Elm Avenues, when they heard the sounds of the city trash truck over in the next alley. As they usually do, they came out of their box to be safe, when the truck operator raised the big, heavy metal dumpster to empty it. To their horror, they saw a good sized turtle very slowly ambling toward them, about halfway from the end of the alley. What concerned the cats was the fact that the turtle was making his way in one of the small valleys of ruts made by vehicles over the years. They knew the approaching truck would squish the turtle. With no time to lose, they ran quickly to the turtle, who paid them no heed, until they began to redirect his progress in a way to get him out of the rut before the heavy truck got there. Then, when they began to try to help him, the turtle promptly pulled his head and legs inside his shell, making him into an oversized hockey puck.

Cats and turtles don't have a common language to allow easy communications, so the cats were at a loss to tell the turtle he was in grave danger. They tried to push him out of the way, but it was like trying to scoot a big rock. Since the turtle's shell was an almost perfect circle, they lifted one side until it was almost vertical, and while two of them kept it balanced, the third cat pushed on the edge and thus rolled the turtle out of harm's way. When the trash truck entered the alley, it ran through a small puddle of muddy water, and

the liquid splashed and squirted out with great force. The three cats shuddered thinking what the truck's big tire would have done to the hapless turtle, if he were still there, where the tire rolled with such weight. Meanwhile, the turtle felt the cats turn him on edge and roll him like a cartwheel, before letting him be left alone. He then heard the truck's engine roar and the truck shaking the ground. He heard the clanking and clanging of the dumpster being raised and dumped and the noise of the doors opening and banging shut. With no vision, since he had his head pulled inside his shell, he imagined the three cats were causing all the noise and commotion.

After ten or so minutes of quiet, the turtle ventured to poke his head outside his shell and look around. Of course, the trash truck was long gone, so he had no understanding of what caused the tempest of loud sounds. When the three cats approached him, he was a bit scared, but they made nice sounds and made moves slowly, as they gently nudged him toward their box where he would be safe. They saw him nibble at some grass at the edge of the pavement, so they went over the fence into the next yard to get some tender vegetation and placed it close to him. They noticed his shell had some areas painted with crayons and fingernail polish, as if some children had been playing with him. When he had eaten some food and drank some water, the turtle felt much better and more trusting of the cats, even if they had made the ground shake and made lots of noise earlier.

The three cats were happy the turtle was feeling better and no longer afraid of them, but they were still concerned for his safety in the alley. They began to discuss where he would be safe and happy, and how to get him moved to some safe place. Soon they were thinking of the courtyard at Havenwood Retirement Village, the rock garden and the fountain pool. They protected and took care of their guest and pondered how to get him to Havenwood. When Alfred came with Fluffy to get the trio to go to Havenwood, the three cats presented their new friend to Alfred. To his credit, Alfred didn't miss a beat as he baby-talked to the three cats and unceremoniously loaded the turtle into the limo and went by to pick up the ladies on their way to visit the people at the nursing home.

When they arrived at Havenwood, Alfred told Miss Primm that he had a friend who would like to become a resident, as he showed her the multicolored turtle. Candy Primm just smiled and winked, as she told Alfred to take the new arrival out to the rock garden. She said she would attend to the paperwork later. The three cats had a good feeling because they had arranged an answer for their turtle friend that served everyone, and made them happy also.

THREE CATS GET JOBS

After the open house of the new Three Cats Service Center, the three namesakes, Alleycat, Tomcat, and Yellowcat, weren't back there for several days. When they happened by, they were greeted like old friends by everyone there. When they entered the area between the service bays and the restrooms, they were surprised to see the little room used by the news media photographers still had their names and pictures there. More than that, they found the snappy little blazers and caps from that photo op session still there on little pegs. Even more, there were dinner bowls with cat food and fresh water placed on the floor, and even a nice big sandbox in the back corner. One of the girls in bookkeeping, Nancy Ledger, came and fussed over the three and put their jackets and hats on them. She then led them into the customer's waiting area, where they created a spontaneous outbreak of approval from the waiting customers.

This reaction from the people awaiting the completion of their car's service served to validate (prove) the value of the three mascots to the business. Tom's wife, Mitzi, had planned for this, when she devised the jackets and hats with the three cats' logo on them. Mitzi has a natural knack for such things and an associate degree in retail marketing from the community college. She and the rest of the staff were very happy to see the way their customers identified with the business' namesake mascots being there at the business. When Mitzi detected signs the three cats were getting restless, after they awoke from midafternoon catnaps, she carefully removed their hats and blazers before they left.

In coming days the three cats found it very convenient and enjoyable to go to "their" business for a nice breakfast set down by Nancy or one of the others, who loved the three cats. Then, if the trio didn't slip away quickly, somebody would dress them in their business uniforms and the three strutted around in the customer's waiting room. One morning with a brisk north breeze, the three were enjoying warm cereal and people were admiring them. One lady customer, who had just dropped off her little sports car, commented on the cats' hearty appetite. Alleycat said to the other two, "Well – it sure beats cold pizza crusts from the dumpster." So ..., the three cats were thus introduced into the world of having a regular – well, almost regular job. When the accountant, Alan B. Numbers, was talking to Mitzi about setting up the expenditures for the materials needed to make the three cats' business wear, the three cats happened to be in earshot and heard the discussion. Mitzi replied to Alan's question by saying the amount was thirty-six dollars for some material, eighteen dollars and twenty cents for some other, and eleven dollars and sixty four cents for miscellaneous supplies. Alan made some entries on his pocket calculator and announced, "That's sixty-five dollars and eighty-four cents." Then he mumbled to himself and entered some additional numbers and said, "The tax is five-forty three, making the total seventy one-twenty-seven. As they discussed the sales tax treatment needing to be listed in a separate column etc., Tomcat laughed and said that not only were the three cats employed now, but were also taxpayers, as well.

The three cats just eased into the habit of going to the service center and enjoying showing off to the customers, while everyone treated them like royalty. They developed the routine of depending on the staff for their food most of the time, because it was easier, cleaner, and better tasting than some of their potluck from the dumpsters. All this – and there was no contending with other cats, dogs, and rats for the better food. Some days one of them might have something on his agenda that precluded his being “on the job” with the others. On days they were scheduled to go with Fluffy and her people to Havenhouse Retirement Village, the crew at the service center understood and allowed for their not being there.

When a strong, winter snowstorm blew into town, Mitzi asked Tom if the three cats could spend the night. Tom called the alarm company and asked about that. The alarm company General Manager, Jeffry Knozlots, assured Tom that the alarm system’s motion detectors were designed to accommodate small pets. To be sure, Jeffry notified the central station manager that this customer was leaving three medium-sized cats inside for the first time. All went well and the three cats stayed out of the snow.

THREE CATS - STOWAWAY TOMCAT

The three cats had been told not to go into the service bay area where mechanics and technicians were working on customers' cars at the Three Cats Service Center. There was too much danger of their being hurt or causing the workers to be hurt in accidents. They pretty much had free rein to go everywhere else and they did so often. A family pulling a trailer loaded with household goods stopped at the service center to get their pickup's brakes serviced. The trailer was unhitched in the fenced parking lot located behind the store. The three cats watched with interest as this was being done. When the family went into the waiting area, Alleycat and Yellowcat followed them, while Tomcat was checking out the cars parked there either waiting their turn in the shop, or waiting for the owners returning to pick up their vehicle. Tomcat noted that the tarp covering the trailer had a small opening near the corner at the rear of the trailer. It was a challenging jump from the fender to the top, and the tarp was somewhat slicker than Tomcat expected, but he made it. By the time he carefully made his way on top, to the place where the tarp had the opening, he was about tuckered out. He eased his way inside the opening and stretched out to rest from his efforts.

It was a cool, cloudy day, and under the tarp it was cozy-warm. Tomcat had just finished his lunch, so his stomach was full ..., and he got sleepy. The hum and sounds of traffic on the streets made a lullaby in Tom's ears, and he drifted off into a deep catnap. When the pickup was returned after a quick adjustment, Tomcat didn't know a thing until the workers connected the trailer to the pickup. When he felt this, Tom became fully alert, but stayed out of sight, since he really shouldn't have been snooping around under the customer's trailer tarp to start with. Speaking of start – that's just what happened; the pickup with the family in it started moving from the parking lot into the street traffic. Tom looked out, intending to jump from the trailer, but the sight of all those cars, and recalling the injuries Alleycat recently suffered in a traffic accident, he decided against it. He thought he could get out at the first place they stopped. That turned out to be the last traffic light before the pickup and trailer entered the onramp to the Interstate Highway. The traffic here was much more dangerous looking to Tomcat, so he eased himself down into the tightly packed home furnishings and found a comfortable place to curl up on a nice soft armchair.

The next time the pickup and trailer stopped was after it exited from the Interstate in another state over two hundred miles from Centerville and the Three Cats Service Center. It was dark and Tomcat returned to his lookout post at the rear of the trailer. The pickup was backing the trailer on a driveway toward an opening garage door at a big white house. The family got out and went into the house, as the driver unhitched the trailer and parked the truck beside the trailer. Tomcat covertly watched, as the people unloaded some bags and stuff from the truck. One of the little ones was drinking from a kiddie cup which reminded Tomcat of how thirsty he was. He let a small "meow" escape from his mouth. Everyone stopped what they were doing and the small boy nearest to the trailer said, "I think I heard a cat," and his sister said, "I know I heard a cat." Thus, the Roberts family discovered Tomcat and gave him water and food and let him explore a really big litter box ..., their new backyard.

Next morning Mrs. Roberts called the number on the invoice she had from the Three Cats Service Center in Centerville. She told the manager that their work on the truck's brakes was good, and that they appreciated the unusual gesture of his company including a real live cat dressed in company togs, but since the cat had such an appetite, they desired to return him. The manager was elated and said they had been looking everywhere for Tomcat. He got the Roberts' address and telephone number and said one of their transports was scheduled to come through there tomorrow and would pick up Tomcat and return him to his job. There was no mention of docking his pay for the unauthorized absence.

Draw a pickup truck pulling a covered trailer.

THREE CATS AND THE BORROWED BALLOON

It was a lazy fall afternoon with clear skies and just a hint of a breeze stirring from time to time. The three cats were resting from a trip to Otto's Meat Market, as they were returning home. They were under a hedgerow bush overlooking a busy street intersection. It was so nice that time of day, and they enjoyed watching the traffic and the pedestrians, as the traffic light signals controlled the ebb and flow. They watched as people gathered at the bus stop until several would be waiting; then a bus would stop and several people would get off and most of those waiting would board the bus. These cycles of activity were repeated over and over, while the lazily resting cats enjoyed watching it all.

They noticed a little old lady with a walker and a small shopping bag come to the intersection and wait for the traffic light to signal her to proceed in the walkway to cross the busy street. They recognized her as one, who lived only a couple of blocks further in the direction she was headed. They could see her hesitate, start to cross, only to abandon her effort and step back to the relative safety of the curb. This concerned Yellowcat, Tomcat and Alleycat, because the turn-right-on-red vehicles and others might not see the small short lady, especially the tall delivery vans and the even taller, jacked up pickup trucks. They knew she didn't have good eyesight in spite of her thick glasses. She was a favorite of theirs because she was always nice to them, when they visited her cat, Gizmo, and her dog, Snarky.

As they watched the panorama of interacting vehicle and people traffic, they discussed the little lady's dilemma and what might be done to help her out. Some twenty or thirty feet from her was a park bench under a big elm tree. Sitting on the bench was a younger lady with a toddler, who had a red helium-filled balloon on a tinseled string about six or eight feet long. They had been there for some time and weren't apparently awaiting a bus. The three cats discussed all these things and formed a plan of action to help the little lady with the shopping bag and walker.

All three cats came from under the big bush and proceeded to where the lady and the toddler with the red balloon were sitting. With the timing of the traffic lights firmly in mind, (all cats are gifted in such things) Yellowcat went directly to the little lady with the walker, while the other two stopped near the little girl and her mother. Yellowcat brushed against the little lady's legs to get her attention, while Alleycat, quick as a wink, took the tinseled string from the child's grasp and he and Tomcat sped to their buddy. They all three began to mingle around the little lady's feet, and as the walk light illuminated, they gently pushed against her fragile legs, urging her to enter the crosswalk. She felt reassured by their presence. With Tomcat and Yellowcat urging her forward, Alleycat preceded them with the balloon floating overhead. This was a traffic stopping thing, as the red balloon with its sparkling-in-the sun string proceeded in front of the lady with her walker and shopping bag. The group arrived safely at the curb just seconds before the light changed and the traffic pattern resumed its prior condition.

Several people who witnessed this strange happening began to clap and call "BRAVO" to the three cats. One lady didn't clap because she was using her cell phone to record the entire event. Of course, she also documented the three cats returning the red balloon to the toddler. Of course, the lady with the cell phone recording was able to get the footage on the six o'clock news at the television station, where she worked in the mail room.

The three cats missed the six o'clock presentation, but the people working at the service center saw it. The next day, they had it on a loop running on the television set in the customer's waiting area. Guess who enjoyed watching it over and over, all day long.

THREE CATS AND THE CONTEST

The three cats, Yellowcat, Tomcat and Alleycat, had been coming to the Three Cats Service Center for breakfast for the past several weeks, since one of the lady service techs had been fixing their morning meal for them there. Young cats can jump up into a dumpster much easier than older cats. Any cat finds it better to have a nice bowl of tasty food at floor level than having to scrounge in the alley with other, strange and sometimes mean cats contesting for the random scraps there. At the service center, one of the young techs fixed a small pet door at the bottom of one of the shop's overhead doors. He installed an electric latch system and attached small plastic tags on each of the three cat's collars. When the latch system detected the presence of one of the tags, it released, and the cat could push the flap door open and come in or go out. Other animals could not push the door open to get in. This made the eating situation much more peaceful and enjoyable for the three cats.

The lady who fixed the three cats' food for them is named Kathryn Castleman, and her friends call her Kitty. She shops for supplies for the employee's coffee breakroom and includes getting food for the service center's namesakes, the three cats. Mostly she bought canned or dry sacked cat food, but she also got special treats like Kitty Bits and catnip. Once she found entry forms packaged with the Kitty Bits, for an essay contest sponsored by the manufacturer. When she had time later, she filled out the entry form and wrote a short essay telling how she enjoyed the taste and texture of their product. She complimented the manufacturer's e-z-pour package and resealable opening that helps keep the remaining stored product fresh. She didn't mention that this feature also kept the strong smell of the product from stinking up the whole building. As a little private joke she signed her entry "Kitty Katt."

A few weeks later the mail at the service center contained an important looking envelope addressed to "Miss Kitty Katt." When Kitty opened it, she found a letter from the manufacturer of Kitty Bits announcing her first prize blue ribbon in the contest. It was signed by the chairman, the president, and the marketing vice president. The letter specified the first place prize was a year's supply of their premier product being shipped to Kitty Katt. There was enclosed with the letter, a fancy certificate with those signatures along with the vice presidents of sales and production affixed. In the center was a space left blank except for the word, "photo." Kitty filled this space with a good photograph of the three cats and posted it on the bulletin board for everyone to enjoy. Of course Kitty's uncle, the mayor saw this and brought it to the attention of the local newspaper people, who ran a big story about it along with pictures of the three cats, the Three Cats Service Center, and Kitty Castleman. They even mentioned that she is the mayor's niece, and that her uncle is on the board of directors at the service center.

Of course, the three cats took all this in stride and stopped bragging about all the fanfare to their cat friends ..., after several months. About the same time, they began to share their ample supply of Kitty Bits since it was stacking up in the warehouse, and they were eating less of it these days, and enjoying other entrees more, such as scraps of food in the cafeteria and items from Otto's Meat Market and the fishing boats down at Fulton's Pier. The certificate was removed by Kitty from the bulletin board and placed with other memorabilia in the storeroom. The mayor remembered it as if it were something he had personally done, just as the three cats did. Last week when Kitty was shopping for supplies for the service center, she had "cat food" noted on her shopping list. She reached for a bag of new cat food, when she saw it advertised an enclosed entry form for entering a contest. Remembering the excitement and extra work caused by the earlier contest entry by her, she moved her eyes and hands to select a less expensive brand that offered no contest to enter. The accounts payable department appreciated the lower cost, and the three cats enjoyed the food, exactly like they do everything Kitty puts in their bowls.

THREE CATS AND THE CIRCUS

Alleycat, Yellowcat and Tomcat, were returning to their cardboard box/home late one summer afternoon after fishing down at the creek. Earlier in the week, they had noticed several trucks with workers on the big grassy meadow at the edge of town. Now they could see there was a very big circus tent set up there and a makeshift parking lot full of cars with people going to and from the big top tent.

With their creels full of fish (Here we're referring to the cats' stomachs; normally a creel is a basketlike container a fisherman uses to store his catch of fish.) the three decided to visit the circus before continuing homeward. They went by the ticket booth at the main entrance, where people were lined up with their money in their hands to buy tickets. Cats don't have hands ..., nor money for that matter. They continued around to the far side of the big tent, where the doors for the circus workers were located. Also located there were two, beefy looking workers with two, mean looking guard dogs. The three cats moseyed on past there and finally found the free cat entrance ..., a place where the edge of the tent was puckered open just the right size to allow a (I started to say sneaky) smart cat to (I almost said slip) squirm underneath. Inside they found themselves in an area beneath the spectator's rows of seats. Lots of dropped popcorn and pieces of hot dogs and hamburgers were there, but the cats weren't too interested, since they were pretty full of fish, thank you.

They worked their way to the front of the seating area, where they could see what the crowd overhead were cheering and clapping about. They almost couldn't believe their eyes with the things they were able to see. There was a man with a chair held in one hand and a long whip in the other. He had three large animals sitting atop big stools surrounding him. It took the three cats a moment to realize those animals were big-BIG cats! The man would crack his whip loudly as he called the monster cats loudly by names and command them to do various tricks for the crowd's amusement. Another man had some cats almost as large with stripes performing jumping tricks, while a tall lady in tights had a dozen or so little dogs yapping, as they were jumping through hoops, climbing ladders, and jumping into a pile of balloons. While all this was going on in three large rings on the floor, there were several very big elephants and horses mounted with girls performing around the outer perimeter of the floor. With all these acts in progress there were some men and women all very slender and dressed in swimsuit looking outfits, performing in the air high overhead. When they thought nothing else could happen, a man climbed a tall ladder to slide feet first into a big cannon barrel. The brass band drummed a crescendo and abruptly stopped as the cannon fired with a loud B O O M and the man flew from its mouth far across the span of space to land in a big net. He rolled like a ball and then, as the crowd held their breaths he bounced up and took a bow. The crowd went wild!

There were so many things going on at once, the three cats felt, even with three pairs of eyes they were missing lots of things. With everyone intensely watching the actions in the arena, nobody even noticed three very small cats under the bleachers. The three cats moved up close beneath the first tier of seats and marveled at the never ending, high-speed delivery of different acts.

The crowd gave a great "OOOH" and were looking up. What they saw was one of the pretty flying trapeze performers swinging, held by only one foot by her muscular man partner. A second man at the opposite pole, timed his leap and took the girl safely to the other side and the crowd really went bonkers. Someone above the three cats was heard asking if that was a planned part of the program or an accident. Someone else said, "What difference does it make?" A third voice chimed in with, "They did it the same way the last two nights." Only then, did the three cats realize it was night outside, since the bright lights inside the big top made it seem to be daytime.

The three cats were finding their way to the "free" cat's entry/exit slit, when they realized how thirsty they had become, while watching everything. They found a discarded ice drink that was almost completely melted and shared it. Then they knew they were much hungrier than when they got there. Those hotdog and burger scraps smelled much more inviting, so they ate some on the way home.

THREE CATS AND THE CIRCUS II

After the three cats got home from their evening at the big tent, they kept talking about all the things they had seen there. Next day they were making the rounds of some of the places they liked to frequent and where they saw some of their friends. That's where they discovered that the biggest cats at the circus were African lions, and the striped cats were Bengal tigers. When they talked to their buddies about the things they had seen, everyone wanted to have a chance to witness it all for themselves. Arrangements were made for several of them to meet at the rear side of the big tent later that afternoon.

The group arrived in ones and twos and stayed out of sight from the occasional circus workers in the area. Then they went from their hiding place in the nearby bushes, and followed one of the three cats to the free cat entrance, and quickly out of sight. Within a half hour there was a cat gallery gathered beneath the front row bleachers. At first there wasn't much to eat there, but in a little while there began to be some popcorn, hamburger and hotdog scraps dropping down from the excited spectators seated above.

The show activities this evening were as exciting as before, and the three got added enjoyment from sharing the experience with their pals from downtown. They wished they could have Fluffy there too, but Mrs. Pennyrich always checked to make sure Fluffy was home every night before the lady would retire for the night. Once, Fluffy was late getting home, and Mrs. Pennyrich had Alfred and the other staff members combing the neighborhood for Fluffy. The cats that were able to be there to take in the show were all so happy that it made up for Fluffy not being there, and the three promised themselves they would take time to tell their rich friend all about it at their first opportunity.

The three had warned their buddies about the terrific roar of the cannon and about the girl on the trapeze being held by only one foot, to be rescued by the second performer, and such. Sure enough, the cannon boomed loudly, and the man flew forth in a great cloud of smoke and landed safely. The big cats and little dogs were in fine form again tonight, and the horses and elephants were prancing and plodding around the arena edge as before. Then the crowd hushed as the girl was caught by her partner by only one foot. The three cats thought to themselves ..., yeah we saw this last night. The second acrobat timed his move and swung into action – he swung toward the others to save the girl. **OH NO NO**, he collided with the two; they all spun around in a blur – and THE GIRL DROPPED, screaming as she fell from the great height!

She fell out of the sight of the lower bleachers and the three cats. Her screams stopped, and there was silence in the crowd ..., then she bounced from her impact with the safety net and bowed to the crowd. Then the ringmaster/announcer appeared beside her, mic in hand to ask the crowd for a round of applause for the performers. That made the three cats think it was all part of the act, since the announcer was on the floor a few minutes earlier. Then they felt their suspicions were proven, when the two men swung from their high perches to drop to the safety net, bounce and stand with the girl and the announcer.

On their way home the three cats talked to their friends about the unusual opportunity they had all enjoyed by seeing the circus acts and the animals. They all agreed that sometimes, just like the acrobat's show, some bad times in life are just preludes to much better things to follow. Someone correctly said that it is darkest just before dawn. When things look hopeless is when not to give up, but to resolve to do everything we can to obtain a good result in the end. Many times it may look as if there is no hope for things to get better, but if we quit trying, we will never know whether they were going to improve or not. House pets look to their human protectors for safety and happiness. Humans must look to their Creator for all good things in this life and our lives hereafter. Some ask if pets go to heaven when they die. I don't know, but I do know that if the Lord wants them to, they surely will.

This story is about the closing act at the circus. The next day the circus people started taking down the big top and packing to move to their next location. The three cats talked about planning to see them again, when they next set up the big tent in Centerville.

THREE CATS AND THE WEDDING

The three cats had noticed that they saw Tom Steele, their attorney friend at Havenwood Retirement Village, quite often, well after he helped Candy Primms with her appearance before the board of directors. Tom enjoyed visiting the residents there and the staff ..., especially Candy. Tom was always nice to the three cats, just as he was with everyone.

Candy and Tom announced their engagement in the spring and planned their wedding for later in the summer. Tom began to spend so much of his time at Havenwood that he occupied a vacant office there, and his law firm had an extension telephone and computer connection installed. The three cats enjoyed being in Tom's office there, since he treated them so well. Sometimes Tom and Candy ate in the dining room with many of the ambulatory residents. Other times the two of them went to eat out, and Penny's assistant, Gwyn, knew she was in charge. She knew to call Candy's cell phone on anything she needed help with. One afternoon that cell phone interrupted the selection of a nice engagement ring at Jethro's Jewelry Store.

When Candy and Tom announced their engagement and planned marriage, it surprised no one. The announcements went out, and everyone agreed the two would make a fine married couple. The three cats were especially happy as events unfolded, because they were on the scene when the couple first met and developed their friendship which blossomed into a tender, caring relationship. In fact, in the three cats' minds, they figured in a big way in helping cause the upcoming wedding. They liked both people, and felt they would like the two together even more. The couple could sense how proud the three cats were of themselves, and how important they thought they were in the way things were developing. With these items being so important to them and the cats, they started thinking of ways the three cats could be included in the wedding service.

As some of the plans were developing and being discussed among friends and family, everyone joined in to include the three cats. The mayor's niece, Mitzi, who designed and produced the three cats' work uniforms for the Three Cats Service Center, made spiffy outfits like tuxedos for the trio, under Candy's guidance. She and Jethro from the jewelry store designed hats for the cats that could contain the rings for the double ring ceremony. The crew at Fire Station #3 started early with cleaning up and trimming the three cats. They all laughed at the changes such treatment made in their favorite cats. Before the clean-up efforts, Alleycat was the worst looking of the three, but with the crew's care his multicolored calico coat was most handsome. The other two also benefited from the treatment, and in their outfits they were a great looking team.

The ceremony was held right there at Havenwood, and the visiting guests and regulars made an impressive crowd. The wedding couple and their attendants stood with the officiating minister as the couple recited their vows. When the minister asked the best man for the rings, he turned and looked up the aisle made by chairs. With this, the three cats came into view, and everyone marveled as the trio in their uniforms, slowly and in perfect unison paraded to the best man. He removed the rings from the cushion hats and presented them to the preacher. The three cats stood stock still until the final "I dos" were said, and the groom kissed the upturned lips of the bride. After the press photographers finished popping flashbulbs, and the bride threw her corsage to her best unmarried friend, the three cats resumed being three cats.

At the reception in the Havenwood dining room, the caterer had placed three small plastic bowls in a corner near the kitchen. Carefully hand painted on the three bowls were the names of each of the three cats. After the reception, the happy couple left to catch their plane that would connect at JFK to take them to their honeymoon in Tom Steele's native Scotland. The three cats, having filled their stomachs on fine food from the little bowls, caught a ride with a resident in her wheelchair to their sleeping quarters in the linen closet. They all agreed they wouldn't want to do this every week. Their pictures in their little tuxedos, are displayed in the trophy case in the entry hall to this day.

THREE CATS GAINING WEIGHT

Mitzi at the Three Cats Service Center was the first to say anything about it, and the first one to suggest something needed to be done about it. "It" was the fact that the three cats were becoming too fat for their own good. She first noted the problem when their uniforms began to be too tight to be comfortable. Mitzi knew the outfits had not shrunk, because she knew the quality of the material she had used and the cleaning methods used to keep the outfits looking fresh and spotless. The problem was most apparent with Alleycat, the one who always wanted seconds of the richest food available. Mitzi knew the responsibility was on the people, who made too much food, too easily available for the three cats. She knew cats living free in their natural habitat are usually not too fat. She realized the fattest felines were the pampered pets, whose caretakers lavish too much rich, calorie-laden food on their pets.

Her concerns were discussed with Candy at the Havenwood Retirement Village, who involved the nutritionist there. As a result the people, who fed the three cats were all put on notice to stop being so good to the trio and start giving them less of more healthy food. Those included in the loop were the people at Fire Station #3, Central Police Precinct Station, the ones at the service center, and at Havenwood. The three cats hardly noticed the changes, as they still had plenty of food to satisfy their appetites and still had the ability to forage for food in all the places they had done all their lives. In natural surroundings animals tend to be self-regulating in food intake. A cat for instance, who gets overweight cannot move as fast to catch prey and cannot climb and move about as well. When a cat cannot access the dumpster because he is overweight, his food intake is affected, thus his own weight is automatically reduced. Any house pet can be overfed to the point of becoming unhealthy. This also applies to human beings, and we can see it in any crowd of people. Go to any hospital, clinic, or doctor's waiting room, and check the ratio of obese to normal weight people to see what is meant here.

As the new regimen was put into effect, the three cats all began to enjoy the results. They became more energetic, alert, and happy as shown by their becoming more like themselves in earlier times. They spent more time visiting people and other animals and spent less time sleeping and just laying around doing nothing. Several people who had noticed the three becoming more sedentary had thought it was caused just by advancing age, but now saw it was related to their extra weight. Some of those who noticed these things, thought how the facts could relate to their own case. Because of this some, who were overweight, decided to do something positive and took action. Someone at Havenwood observed that not everyone has the physical strength to do push-ups, but anyone can muster the moral strength to do pushbacks from the table when they have eaten enough.

Of course, the three cats are like us, in that as they advance in age, they tend to not be as active as they were when they were younger. If all cats acted like kittens all their lives, it would change the cat kingdom's place in the animal world. Likewise, if human beings continued to act like children all their lives it would create lots of problems. Look at the liberals running Hollywood for instance. As the three cats become older, they become wiser and more careful not to be doing dangerous things that result in injuries. That is normal for all animals, including God's premier animal, man, whom He created in His own image. It's okay for age to slow us all down a bit, but we shouldn't unnecessarily penalize ourselves by having to tote around unneeded, unhealthy baggage. The Bible tells us at 1 Corinthians 3:19, that we are to take care of our bodies. That includes eating right, getting exercise, and not doing anything hurtful to our body, mind, or spirit.

The three cats never even realized their caretakers were doing good things for them to help them be healthy and happy. This is also true of us, as our Caregiver looks after our happiness, health, and our soul's salvation for eternity.

THREE CATS AND FRIENDS GO SOUTH

Last year the three cats, Alleycat, Tomcat and Yellowcat, took a trip, going upstream of the creek, where they sometimes go fishing. After they returned home, they often talked and recalled some of the best parts of that adventure. Sometimes they mused about the possibility of exploring downstream, where the creek joins a much larger river that flows to the bay connecting to the ocean. When their cousin, Bobbycat, was visiting them, they were remembering that great adventure, and Bobbycat was very interested in hearing all about it. Someone mentioned that they had talked about going downstream some day, and Bobbycat really got excited.

Later the four of them were talking about family matters and the bad feelings between Bobby and another cousin, Pepe Phew, entered into the talk. As sometimes happens, the subjects became intermixed, and a dream plan developed about inviting Pepe to go with the four to explore the creek and river someday. Bobby and Pepe had not been close cousins after a heated discussion at a family reunion a few years back, and since the three cats liked both of them, they were hoping to see things get better.

As things developed more in their dream trip, an event occurred that put more form and substance in their plans. Four boys had been using a raft made by two of their dads from mostly scrap lumber, to float out in the creek while playing at being pirates. The three cats heard the boys saying they were tiring of using the raft, as they discussed their families' vacation plans. With this in mind, the three cats discussed with Bobby the possibility of using the raft for their venture downstream. They doubted their ability to get the raft unmoored from the bank due to its size. When they mentioned all this to their big dog friend Brutus, he went down to the creek to inspect the raft with the cats' plans in mind. When Brutus checked it out, he opined he could easily loosen the rope and by perhaps getting a little wet, get the raft afloat. Brutus also hinted that the cats might find a big dog a useful shipmate even after the raft was launched. Brutus wasn't too concerned about getting a little wet, because he is half Labrador, and that dog breed is right at home in the water.

Remembering their trip up the creek last year, the three cats began to bring some things they would need for the planned trip down to the raft, and put them in the small tarp tent to protect them. They also sent a message by a friend to Pepe, to see if he would be interested in going with them and explained that Bobby wanted him to come along. The next time the three cats were visiting Brutus at Mrs. Pennyrich's mansion, he more than hinted about being included with the adventurers, even saying he had some packages of pet food he wanted to donate to the cause, even if there wasn't "enough room" for him to go along with them. The three cats discussed this among themselves, trying to think of reasons why it might not be a good idea. They all knew Brutus was a reliable helper and careful to always do his part, or more. They took a vote, and it turned out that all three thought it would be great to have Brutus come with them. Brutus was delighted. His stablemate, Fluffy, the family show cat was appalled. Brutus began taking stuff for the planned trip down to the raft and guarding it during times when people were fishing or visiting in the creek area.

Pepe showed up and was excited about the trip and trying to be nice to Bobby, who was also on his best behavior. On the appointed morning, the six adventurers gathered at the raft and put their last minute things aboard. It was a nice clear morning with a gentle west wind that promised clear skies for the next few days. The smaller cats all got aboard, and Bobby pushed the front of the raft with his head, while Brutus waded into the shallow water with the tether line in his mouth. When all was ready, the cats aboard the raft all went to the aft end to get their weight off the grounded prow and on the part that was afloat in the water. With an "Arf-arf" from Brutus, Bobby pushed with all his might while Brutus tugged on the rope. With a cheer from those aboard the craft, it slid smoothly into the creek. Bobby had to make a long leap to gain the raft, and Brutus swam for a short time until the raft was caught in the current and started moving downstream. Brutus swam alongside, and Tomcat took the rope from him. Then, the soaking wet dog pulled himself aboard and stood, and like all wet dogs, shook himself violently. This resulted in five more soaked animals ..., five soaked and very happy animals.

The creek's current was slow, and the raft almost ran aground a couple of times the first hour, but passing a point where another creek joined and then later a spot where a large spring emptied into the creek, the flow increased. By noon, they had passed the last buildings in the warehouse sector of town and were floating through farming country. They began to see more wildlife along the banks of the widening creek and occasional anglers fishing where a roadway bordered the water. The water was now deeper and running with a stronger, faster current. They approached a bridge where auto traffic was crossing overhead. At first they were concerned if the span was high enough for their raft to clear, but as they got closer, it was apparent the bridge was plenty high enough to even clear the flag pole from which the kids had flown their Jolly Roger flag. It was quiet most of the time, and they could hear people's voices and machinery running on the farms. Then they heard a sound ahead that they couldn't identify; a low rumbling sound. Bobby jumped atop the cabin to get a better view ahead, and announced that he could see white water ahead as if there were rapids or a waterfall!

The animals all started securing all loose items on deck into the cabin and placing themselves in the safest places they could get in order to prepare for whatever was ahead. Bobby jumped down and he and Brutus positioned themselves at the two corners of the prow where they might be able to keep the raft from colliding with any rocks or other threats. The sound of the rushing, cascading water became louder and louder. Then the raft made a sidewise jerk and turned quickly to a sidewise attitude and the port (left) side dipped low, and some water flooded aboard. Just as quickly the starboard (right) side dipped and quickly rose high and scraped on a big boulder as the prow fell low, and those aboard could see green and white water ahead. The entire raft dropped suddenly and smacked the water or rocks so hard it shook and groaned. Lots of water washed aboard. Then as the water ran off the deck, the raft was in calm water and spinning slowly so everyone could look back where they had been to see the expanse of white, foaming water and boulders. They couldn't believe they had come through that giant carwash unscathed.

The waterway was now much wider and flowing more slowly. It didn't really look much like a creek anymore, but more like what would be called a river. The raft was in the main current, near the center, and things aboard were drying out nicely. One of the cats asked how far it might be where they would join the river. Someone opined this might be the river after the rapids. Soon thereafter, all questions were answered as they saw ahead a vast expanse of water with a big tugboat pushing much bigger barges. As their little raft began to enter the river, they could see the water was less cloudy and clearer, while being bluer and deeper. When they were floating near midstream the banks were quite a distance from them. Two fishermen in a bass boat passed them on the starboard side and waved as their powerful outboard motor made a throaty roar and the boat made spray fly at every little wave.

They passed beneath a big bridge with lots of vehicles going both ways. This bridge was higher above the river than the highest office building in Centerville, which they knew was sixteen floors high. Just past this bridge was a lower one with a train crossing the river on a railroad track!

The river flowed somewhat more slowly than the creek and gave them more time to sightsee and point out to one another the different things slowly moving by in a constant panorama. It also gave them time to think of other things. Things like what's going on back home. The three cats thought of things at the Three Cats Service Center, and how things were going for the people at Havenwood Retirement Village. Bobbycat thought of his family, and wondered how things were with them. Pepe thought of the little den of skunks he was so far away from. Brutus thought of Mrs. Pennyrich, Alfred and Fluffy and if they might be missing him and worrying about his safety. They all thought of the fact that they were in a world they had never even dreamed about. A world with no dumpsters, no pet food bowls, no grasshoppers or mice to catch. All this was bearing on their minds because their food supply was getting pretty thin and pretty soaked by their trip through the rapids. This water wonderland was beautiful and interesting, but it was very interrupting of their usual routines. Well, one thing was the same, they could take a nice nap anytime they wanted to, and there was plenty of fresh drinking water.

One of the tugboat captains reported the raft to the coast guard as a hazard to navigation, saying there were some dogs and cats aboard, but no human being visible. The local sheriff's river patrol heard this radio transmission and volunteered to check it out since the coast guard didn't have a vessel in the area. When the deputies pulled up beside the raft, they saw the reports were accurate because the dog and cats were not accompanied by anyone. The men lashed their patrol boat to the raft and spoke to the animals. Brutus barked and wagged his tail to show his approval of the men's actions. The patrol boat slowly returned to their dock with the raft in tow. The fellow officers there laughed and said the raft occupants couldn't be charged with operating a watercraft without proper license, because the raft failed to meet the standards. They made friends with the unlikely crew from the raft and took them inside their small office. They checked their tags and found Brutus had a telephone number for Centerville on his gold-plated tag. The three cats had similar telephone numbers with the name and address of Fire Station #3 there. They gingerly checked Bobbycat for a tag, while discussing just what kind of cat he was. They observed Pepe at a distance and all agreed they knew what kind of cat he was.

When they called the fire station and reported they had found the animals on an old raft in the river, the dispatcher who took the call was very excited and yelled for someone to tell the fire chief the three cats were located and safe. When Brutus was mentioned, the dispatcher told someone to tell the police that Mrs. Pennyrich's dog was safe too. When told about Pepe, the dispatcher asked if they were sure a skunk was part of the group or maybe just happened to get on the raft. Everyone was glad to hear of the three cats and Brutus being found safe, but no one was even aware Bobbycat and Pepe were with them. Since the three cats and Brutus were valuable to someone, and Bobby and Pepe were sticking with them, the entire group were put up, down at the stables where the sheriff's office kept their mounted patrol horses. The kindly couple, who cared for the horses both happily took the raft crew under their wings, and fed them and made them feel welcome.

After a few days there, and after the local news media people had visited, arrangements were made for a deputy, who had official business in Centerville, to return all six of the animals home. This deputy borrowed a K9 officer's vehicle, outfitted for carrying dogs and brought the raft crew back to Fire Station #3 where the mayor, and many others welcomed them home. As soon as the television crew rolled up their cables, Pepe and Bobby told the three cats they were slipping away to go to the three cats' cardboard box/home to rest for their return to the country tomorrow. Alfred arrived with Mrs. Pennyrich and Fluffy to get Brutus. The three cats were so happy to be back home, and they agreed they would not be concerned in the future with where their creek came or went.

The people at Havenwood and those at the service center were happy their favorite cats were back home. The three favorite cats were even happier.

Can you draw a raft floating in the water?

THREE CATS AND THE KITTENS

The three cats had just settled in at their cardboard box/home and were recounting their day to one another. They had been together for the morning at the Three Cats Service Center, and after their catnap had gone their separate ways for the afternoon. As they were swapping stories, they heard a vehicle enter their alley from Elm Avenue. This was a car they weren't familiar with, and it stopped briefly at the dumpster in front of their abode. Something was tossed into the open dumpster, and the car kicked up some gravel as it quickly departed and made a slight squeal of its tires as it turned onto Cherry. As silence returned to the area, the three cats wondered among themselves as to what might have been discarded from the car into the trash dumpster. They didn't have to wonder very long. At first, they thought they were hearing a kitten mewing somewhere in one of the houses on either side of the alley. This puzzled them since they knew of no kittens anywhere around. Cats tend to keep tabs on such things. Tomcat stuck his head outside to get a better idea of where the mewing was coming from.

He listened intently for a while and pulled his head back inside and announced that the mewing was coming from the dumpster.

This was exciting ..., and concerning news. The three cats quickly got themselves up on the dumpster and down inside. They were looking for a kitten; what they discovered were three little kittens - three very young, little kittens, who barely had their eyes open. More than being so young, the three kittens were weak from hunger, so weak only the largest one was trying to meow. This concerned the three cats as they got busy moving the kittens from the cold dumpster into their warm box. The one making sounds changed his tune from "help us" to "thank you," and the other two stopped squirming and they all three became quiet. It seemed as if they knew instinctively that they were in good hands with the three cats. What to do? The three cats were trying to decide their best course of action. They wanted to wait until morning to take action, but they felt the kittens were at risk of starving, especially the two smaller little girl kittens.

They discussed taking them to the fire station, the service center, or the police station. They knew it would be hard to get any attention from those people at this time of night. Even though it was somewhat farther, they decided on going to Havenwood Retirement Village, where staff members were usually alert at nighttime for the needs of the elderly residents. They devised a plan, where two of them would take a kitten, while one of them stayed with the others in the box. This would allow the two to spell one another off in carrying their kitten, since it was a long trip to Havenwood. This also provided one unburdened cat available for security and safety, since the nighttime was dangerous due to stray dogs and cats roaming about. Tomcat and Alleycat took the weakest little kitten and started to Havenwood, while Yellowcat remained with the other two.

There was still quite a bit of traffic on the streets as the two scurried toward Havenwood. The one with the kitten followed the other one, and they were being as careful as they could, while moving with a sense of urgency. When they got there, they scratched on the security guard's door and the guard opened it and was happy to see them, but concerned for the kitten. He took the kitten in his big hands and took her into the garage to a box of clean wipe cloths. While he was busy getting a nurse, the two cats started home for another kitten. In this manner, the three cats arrived with the boy kitten just after midnight at Havenwood. The people there were working to get a little water and food into the kittens, and were relieved to see the three big cats take a break to eat a little themselves. The people knew this signaled the end of the transfer effort for the night. Seeing the little ones in good hands, the three cats snuggled in a warm corner on some soft packing and started to get some well-earned sleep.

In the days to come, the three cats stayed around the nursing home to be able to see the progress of the new residents. Those three bounced to life under the care of the people. Bounced is a good description, as they playfully bounced around the area set aside for them by the staff members. Tony, the handyman, fixed the kittens a nice plywood enclosed place, where they were happy and restricted from bouncing in dangerous areas. We can probably plan to name them soon.

THREE CATS AND CHANGING TIMES

The three cats have been in the news, so to speak, for several years now and have become well known in Centerville. Most people who read the local newspaper, listen to local radio, and/or watch the six o'clock television news, know about them. The mayor loves to get his picture taken with the three cats as often as there is an excuse for it. The law enforcement and firefighter people think of the three as honorary members of their organizations. They are favorite pets of Mrs. Pennyrich, the community's best known public benefactor. They have attended director's meetings for the board at Havenwood Retirement Village, are welcomed at the big hospital as guests of the chaplain there, and the new Three Cats Service Center is named after them. Even when the circus comes to town, the three cats and their friends are guests of honor, and they are given free passes to all performances.

The three cats have enjoyed very good health for their entire lives, and they have had extra-ordinary living conditions, considering they are after all, alley cats, living by their wits. As the trio became older, and it became more and more difficult for them to forage for food, their circumstances improved. They now have food available six days a week at the service center and seven days per week at Havenwood. The people at Fire Station #3 fixed their cardboard box/home with a heavy plastic wrap that keeps it dry for them. They are welcome to spend the night anytime they wish at half a dozen good places around town. Life has become much easier for the three cats as they enter into their golden years. People undergo similar changes if they are blessed with good circumstances in their elder years. We can see some of these truths in the Bible. In the first book of the Bible, we see at Genesis chapter one, that the Creator of everything, God, created both man and all animals on the sixth day of creation. That would be on Friday of the first week. A few places to see how human beings and their animal friends are provided for by Him, are at Matthew 6:26 and 10:29-31, and in Luke chapter 12.

The three cats look to other animals and especially human beings to help them and provide their needs. The Scriptures tell us in the passages cited above, how God provides for the fish, land animals, and birds. He uses people many times to get these things done for the animals He loves. He wants us to help one another, and He tells us so many times in His instruction manual for mankind, the Bible. Many members of the community in Centerville helped the three cats from the time they were born. As we have seen in reading their stories, the three cats have returned the favors over the years by doing good deeds for their neighbors. That's what Jesus was telling us when He said we are to love our neighbors at Mark 12:31. He even told us to love our enemies at Matthew 5:44.

As the three cats become older and wiser, they spend much of their time helping younger friends benefit from the three cats' experiences and thus avoid some of the bumps and hard spots they had to learn the hard way. This kind of exchange of wisdom allows each generation to bypass some of the mistakes of earlier people and live happier, more useful lives. The three still make their home in the same cardboard box behind the dumpster in the alley, between Cherry and Elm Avenues. They still go to the docks sometimes, when the fishing fleet brings in the day's catch. They still check by Otto's Meat Market and behind the pizza places. They still go to the creek to fish and check the garbage containers behind the big church on fellowship night. If they don't feel like making some of their old rounds or go by the fire station or police station, they know they can count on a no-effort meal at the service center during business hours, or at the kitchen at Havenwood almost any time. They have most of their old friends, and meet new ones almost every day. Times have changed, and so have the three cats. Even when times and conditions change for the worse, the three cats look for ways to cling to the wisdom they have gained over the years and turn events in their own lives to be better for themselves and those around them.

Can you sketch an older cat and a young kitten?

THREE CATS HELP YAP - YAP

The three cats, Tomcat, Yellowcat, and Alleycat, live in a big cardboard box located behind the trash dumpster about midway, between Elm and Cherry in the alley. There are homes on either side of the alley, with fences separating the properties from the alley. One of the houses is where the Martins live with their loudmouthed dog, Yap-Yap. The three cats have never liked Yap-Yap very well, because he starts yapping every time he sees, hears or smells a cat. The Martins have a concrete block fence that is perfect for the cats to walk and sit on. They can't use it much because when Yap-Yap even thinks he detects a cat atop the fence, he starts a loud yipping. The Martins never try to get him to stop his din, but act as if they don't even hear it. The only time when Yap-Yap is quiet, is when the family car goes somewhere and he goes along. Even if Yap-Yap is sleeping in his dog house, if a cat goes down the alley he is up and yapping until the cat clears the alley. To sum it up, that yapping dog has always been a pain in the neck for the three cats.

Last summer the Martins took a long vacation trip, including an ocean liner cruise where no pets were allowed. They arranged with a homeowner's service company to mow their grass, pick up their mail, and feed their dog while they were to be gone. They left plenty of dog food for the service company to put in Yap-Yap's bowl, loaded the car, and left for their three-week holiday. The person at the service company made a coding error showing the field personnel to mow the front yard grass weekly and pick up the mail at the same schedule. The space to be checked for attending to pets was missed. After a few days the little, loud dog began to be hungry. When the man came to mow the front yard grass, Yap-Yap excitedly tried to get his attention, but the man was busy with getting his mower unloaded and set up. He already knew the Martins' dog was a constant barker, so he paid no attention as he started the noisy machine.

The three cats were, of course, unaware of the things over the fence, since the Martins and their dog had never been friendly to them. They did notice Yap-Yap wasn't so loud and aggressive with his yapping. Then a strange thing happened; a stray cat came walking atop the Martins' fence and Yap-Yap just yipped twice and quit. When the stray cat wandered off elsewhere, Yellowcat jumped up on the fence and saw Yap-Yap was near his dog house lying down with his tongue hanging out of his mouth. He hardly noticed Yellowcat and made no move or any sound except a weak whine. This was enough difference to alert the three cats that there was some kind of problem, so they all jumped to the top of the fence and down to the tall grass backyard. They went to the dog and could see he was thin and lanky, with a dry nose and reddened eyes. He attempted to greet them, but was too weak to do much. He had some muddy water, or watery mud where a faucet was slowly dripping. He had a food bowl lying near his doghouse, but not a drop or crumb of food in it. The three cats started a concerted effort to get some food, any kind of food for Yap-Yap. First, they brought over the fence every scrap of old pizza crusts and hamburger leavings they had in their box. Then they began to find whatever they could nearby. Yap-Yap was eagerly eating every scrap of whatever food the three brought him.

Since cats don't have hands or pockets, everything they brought was held in their mouths, which didn't concern Yap-Yap in the least. He ate everything just like it had been unwrapped or opened by someone wearing food serving gloves. Yap-Yap got better in a hurry and showed his appreciation by happily licking his friends, who had come to his aid in his time of need. The three joked that they should be careful about his licking them, since he was eating everything in sight. In the days to come the three cats spent much of their time scrounging for and bringing food to Yap-Yap. He regained his lost weight and became his old feisty self, yapping in glee every time they brought him more good eats.

Yap-Yap now saw his feline friends in a new light and felt a warm friendship with them. He knew, and the three cats knew, but no one else had a clue. When the Martins returned from their long outing, they found Yap-Yap looking really good and really happy to see them. Mr. Martin, seeing the dog food sack in the garage still full, remarked that the service company even supplied their dog's food needs themselves. Yap couldn't tell him differently. The cats were glad to see their neighbors home.

THREE CATS RETURNING FAVORS

The three cats have always had lots of people and other animals go out of their way to be nice and caring to them. They practice that style with one another and with others. Without knowing it they practice the "Golden Rule" given to humanity by Jesus. This can be found at Matthew 7:12, and basically instructs us to treat everyone like we want to be treated by them. This is one of the easiest things to understand and do. Sometimes we want to do others dirty to teach them a lesson or to get even with them, but such things are bad, and work against us most of the time. Divine instructions on this are given in the Bible at Deuteronomy 32:35 and Romans 12:18-20. When we are treated fairly and nicely, we naturally want to return these things with nice, friendly gestures. Many bad dogs respond well to kindness and love. That is not true of all bad dogs. Many grumpy, hard to please people melt into kindness when shown love and consideration. That also, isn't true of all grouches.

The three cats learned as kittens that people and other animals act differently according to whether you are being nice or being nasty. Tomcat learned that Herr Otto at the meat market was always nice to them when they were at his dumpster. When Tomcat slipped through the ajar back door, Herr Otto used a big broom to emphasize his "ABHAUEN!!"

Watch some house cats at a dish or bowl of food. If a new arrival rushes up and starts pushing his way forward, you see and hear hisses and paw swats. On the other hand, if the newcomer meows and waits, the others will likely allow him in by making room. This is not universally true, there are exceptions. Human beings have a God-given conscience to guide them in dealing with one another, and Christians have the always-right directives of our Lord. The Bible tells us the meek shall inherit the earth at Psalms 37:11 and Matthew 5:5. Some animals are less gracious than others. Hogs and dogs, for instance usually can be depended upon to act selfishly, almost as bad as some human politicians. If you have ever had pets, did you favor the bully of the litter, or the runt? See what we're talking about?

The three cats often think of others before themselves, and people admire that in them. When someone befriends the three cats, they usually try to think of ways to repay their benefactors. This is a noble animal instinct. It has been observed in wild animals, such as the occasional dolphin which helps a swimmer to reach safety. Many are the times that pet dogs have saved people from house fires. The three cats learned to be compassionate and helpful from seeing such behavior on the part of others. Sometimes a parent may tell a young family member not to act as some person seen doing wrong. In other words, we can do better ourselves by not emulating someone, who is doing wrong by being a poor example. Acts of kindness don't necessarily have to be great gestures, sometimes they can be small acts of kindness, such as an encouraging smile or pat on the back of a timorous person. At Matthew 10:42, Jesus tells us that even the giving of a cup of cold water to a little one will be rewarded. As you may have noticed, the three cats have been often mentioned, as giving water to those whom they have aided in past stories.

Good deeds are rewarded by those helped by them and by observers, who see them. The three cats are encouraged by many authority figures such as Sgt. O'Malley and the police officers, the personnel at Fire Station #3, the city mayor, news people, and others. Human beings are often encouraged, when they do good deeds that come to public notice. We are also rewarded whenever we do small things for other people's benefit that are only known by few. Sometimes these little acts of goodness are known only to the benefactors, sometimes not even by them. When we do well, we know it; and we receive a good feeling in our inner being. Those whom have accepted Jesus' offer of eternal pardon, paid by His blood, try to always do well because of Him and His expectations for us. We might think of this as repaying a VERY BIG favor by very small ones. Actually no favor – nothing is possible to repay His sacrifice for us. Just as the three cats want to repay favors by good actions, the followers of Christ should always strive to not do anything that might even give the appearance of evil and grieve His Holy Spirit. * * * **This message approved by the three cats.** * * *

THREE CATS AND THE SQUIRREL

The three cats had just finished fishing in the creek down behind the big church and were returning home with full stomachs, when they came to the big oak tree. It was hot and the large, cool shaded area beneath the majestic tree was so inviting. The three sprawled out on the soft grass to enjoy a nice, restful catnap. Thus, they were sound asleep when – THUNK – a big acorn hit the ground in their midst. Well after all, they all thought, we are under an oak tree, and oak trees drop acorns sometimes. Then THUNK THUNK, two more big acorns fell, with one narrowly missing Yellowcat's head. Then they heard the chattering of squirrels directly overhead. They looked up, but could only see tree leaves. Cats don't speak squirrel language, but the three could tell the ones overhead were laughing gleefully at the cat's predicament. Everyone enjoys laughing, but few enjoy being laughed at. There were no acorns falling elsewhere under the big tree, and the ones that were dropping were all narrowly missing hitting them. Then – BONK- a big acorn smacked Tomcat on the top of his head. Tomcat yowled in pain, and the squirrels chattered in glee. This was not funny to the three cats, and they reacted in unison. The three ran swiftly to the big tree trunk and quickly began climbing upward toward the devilish squirrels.

On the ground a fast cat can overtake an average squirrel, with the cat's advantage increasing with the length of the race. Both animals can climb trees, but most squirrels make the average cat look pretty clumsy maneuvering among tree limbs. When the three cats had problems finding the troublemakers, the little imps chattered to give clues as to where they were hiding. Then, when the cats worked their way closer to the squirrels, they would chatter gleefully and scamper elsewhere, just having a gay old time. When crowded and wishing to escape, a squirrel can scamper quickly down a vertical or slanting limb headfirst. Cats must back down a steep limb, thus slowing their progress. When the squirrels tired of making fun with their pursuers, they simply scampered quickly down to the ground chattering in glee enroute to another, nearby tree. One big squirrel remained above the cats daring them to try to catch him. Tomcat, with his head still throbbing from the acorn bomb, felt it was his opportunity and his responsibility to give the smart aleck a good thumping, so he took the challenge and pursued him. The squirrel sped out on an almost horizontal limb, and Tomcat thought he had the tormentor cornered. The squirrel went further and further out on the tapering, smaller limb. Tomcat was hugging the limber limb and carefully getting closer and closer to his quarry.

As Tomcat got closer, he was concentrating on maintaining his balance and grip on the tapering limb, as he thought of the thumping he was planning for the squirrel. Then the squirrel did a most unsportsmanlike thing; he nonchalantly and expertly leaped to another limb almost fifteen feet distant.

His sudden departure caused the long, limber limb Tomcat was left hugging for dear life, to shake and sway violently. The squirrel's graceful leap was a beautiful sight. Tomcat's awkward clinging to the whipping and swaying limb was a fearful sight to the other two cats as they watched and hoped he would be able to cling successfully until the limb stabilized. When it did stop swaying, Tom had to very carefully begin backing toward the thicker, easier-to-grip section of limb. To make this more embarrassing, the trees surrounding the big oak resounded with scores of squirrels chattering to one another in victory celebration.

When the three cats were all safely on the ground they glumly started home. As they were walking beneath another oak tree a big acorn fell, almost hitting Alleycat. None of the three even looked up ..., even when the chattering started. In days to come they made it a practice to not catnap under oak trees unless they could be under some protection from falling or dropped objects. When the other two asked Tomcat about getting even with that big squirrel, he quotes what they all heard the pastor at the big church tell his flock "Vengeance is not ours." They both hear Tom, but they're not sure he means it.

THREE CATS VISIT THE THREE KITTENS

The three little kittens were left in the good hands of the staff at Havenwood Retirement Village and grew like weeds, as the saying goes. The three cats, Alleycat, Tomcat and Yellowcat, visited them frequently and helped the little ones to know just how cats are supposed to act. The residents at the nursing home loved the playful kittens and named them. The boy kitten they called Tinker, and the two girl kittens were named Tiki and Tyke. Someone remarked that the names "suited the three kittens to a T." Sometimes, as kittens tend to do, the three kittens caused problems with their youthful antics. Candy Primms, the boss lady at Havenwood, sometimes wished the full-of- energy trio were somewhere else.

A young married couple, Harry and Sandi Green, who were born and raised there in Centerville had moved to Sandi's uncle's ranch in Idaho, where they had started a successful real estate and insurance business. When they returned to Centerville, to visit Harry's elderly aunt at Havenwood, they saw the three cats there and the three kittens as well. Sandi just fell in love with all six of the felines, especially with the three kittens. When Candy saw the attraction between Sandi and the growing kittens and remembering the mess they caused last week, when they overturned the painter's paint bucket, she talked to Sandi and Harry. When the two were ready to return to the ranch in Idaho, they took the three kittens with them.

The three cats missed their three little, but growing, troublemakers, but were glad to see them go with such nice people as the Greens. A year later the Greens returned to visit his aunt and left the now grown kittens back at the ranch. They parked their big motorhome under the tall oak trees in the Havenwood parking lot, where there were hookup facilities for RVs. Of course, since it was a new thing there, the three cats were compelled to check it out. Sandi saw the three cats eyeing the motorhome, so she opened the door and invited them in. The three cats always liked her and Harry because they were always so very nice and friendly. They all three scampered up the steps into the big palace-on-wheels to explore further.

When Harry returned to the motorhome, he wanted to take it downtown to the Three Cats Service Center to have the windshield washer system serviced. He and Sandi discussed whether to take the three cats with them or leave them. They watched the three looking at a Friskies ad on the television, and Harry chuckled, "Since the service center is named after these three loafers, let's see if they will be happy to go with us." Harry did the unhooking necessary and then cranked the rear-mounted diesel engine. The three cats hardly noticed. When the big rig started moving, the three noticed, but taking a cue from the Green's relaxed manner, they just stretched out on the plush carpet and kept watching the television. When the motorhome pulled into the truck service bay and the door was opened, the three cats hopped down the steps as if they owned the place.

The three cats enjoyed themselves at the service center, as they always do, and when the motorhome was ready to return to Havenwood, they scampered up the steps just as if they owned that too. On the return trip to the nursing home, the Greens marveled at the way the three cats had taken to traveling in the motorhome. This led to discussing taking the three with them to visit the three, now grown up, kittens. When the big motorhome left Centerville a few days later, the three cats were inside, living in the lap of luxury.

The cats, (all six,) were delighted when the three cats arrived at the big ranch house near Soda Springs, Idaho. The three younger cats showed the three older ones around the place. The three cats saw many new things they had never heard of before. They all six went with the ranch foreman when he took the jeep and visited ranch hands working all over the vast ranch. His collie dog, Ruffo, accepted and protected the cats, as if they were family. The cats all remembered the night the little ones were rescued from the dumpster and taken, one at a time, to the safety of Havenwood by the three older cats. Such recall caused the three cats to wonder how things were going back in Centerville. At the same time Harry and Sandi were planning to have the three cats returned home, when the company airplane made a business trip back east next week.

That trip would make a good story for some mothers and dads to spin for young ears in days to come. Perhaps they could put that yarn in print with several others and publish another book. The authors of this little book would be pleased if the title might be something in the order of, "Three Cats Tales Sequel." Oh yeah – and they all lived happily ever after.

THREE CATS AND THE COIN

The three cats were engaging in their favorite pastime, dumpster diving, one nice spring morning, after they had enjoyed a good breakfast at the fire station. The firefighters had some meat loaf that was a little past its prime, and put it down where the three could enjoy it, and enjoy it they surely did. They left there and were alley exploring in the general direction of home, when they found a dumpster that was usually carefully kept closed. The reason cats prefer to travel in alleys rather than streets is because the auto traffic is much less and slower, thus much safer in alleys. Getting back to the open dumpster - they saw the strong March wind was from a direction to help keep the big metal cover opened. They found the cavernous container less than half full of mostly discarded household trash, with no food included. They were about ready to leave, when Alleycat found a big silver coin in a clear plastic protector envelope, among some old letters and papers.

The three cats kept the heavy coin and took it home with them, knowing it had some value, and not knowing how to find the legal owner. They discussed this unusual find among themselves that night. Next morning, remembering the excellent breakfast at the fire station, they took the shiny coin in its protective sleeve to the station. There they made sure to display the coin to several people in the break room, insuring that no one person would be tempted to keep it for himself. The crew were intrigued and called the police precinct to turn the found treasure over to them with the attendant problem of returning it to the rightful owner. An officer stopped by later and took custody of the coin and thanked the firefighters. When the officer turned in the coin and filed his report mentioning the three cats' involvement, it was turned over to the detective division, where it was assigned to a new member of that office. This was detective trainee, Mary Harper, and it was her first solo case. She looked on the assignment as being important. She found just how important, when she showed the coin to patrol Officer Jimmy Blake, who is a coin collector.

Jimmy returned the coin to Mary with a grin and told her to not lose it because it was an 1881-O Morgan silver dollar worth over two thousand dollars. Mary took the still-encased coin to the property clerk, with its paperwork, and told the crime lab she wanted the coin checked for any DNA or other clues that might help in determining ownership. The lab people got the coin from the property room and unsealed the envelope and carefully swabbed the serrated edge of the coin. They carefully swabbed the interior of the envelope itself and sent the swabs to the police crime lab in Capitol City. Since this was a low priority case, they assigned a no-rush code on it and detective Mary Harper turned her attention to trying to determine where the coin had first surfaced. This led to Mary visiting the three cats. She showed the coin in its envelope to the three and baby talked to them asking where they had found this item. The three liked Mary and her caring demeanor with them. They led her to the dumpster and sat down, as if to tell her, "Here."

In time, the crime lab reported the swabs Mary had submitted contained three different DNA specimens, with two of those being blood-related kinfolks. With this important help, Mary investigated the residents of the neighborhood that would use the dumpster where the coin was discovered. She quickly learned the elderly Simmons couple had lived nearby, and that Mr. Simmons was an avid coin collector. The couple had moved to Havenwood Retirement Village and the family home had been sold recently. Mary contacted The Simmons and arranged for a police lab tech to stop by and take cheek swabs for comparison. The resulting lab report showed a positive match with the DNA taken from the Morgan silver dollar. The new owners of the old Simmons home signed off from claiming ownership and the three cats were brought by Mary and her supervisor to see the return of the valuable coin to the rightful owners. The three cats were happy. Mary was happy. The Simmons were very happy, and thankful for everyone's hard work and honesty.

Sketch a big silver dollar. Remember the edges are serrated.

THREE CATS PLUGGING THE JUG

"Putting the plug in the jug" is a country way of saying, finishing a chore – completing an assignment – ending a job. We use it here to indicate this is the closing curtain, the last of this series of three cat stories in this book. It has been the authors' goal to present entertaining little stories for little ears and eyes teaching little truths of happy living using three little cats and their improbable little forays. These essays are meant to be suitable for reading to preschoolers and for early primary students to read to themselves and their peers. Each story contains one or more moral concepts, hopefully without condoning or approving of any serious infractions of good order or humility.

The language is, for the most part, kept simple and direct; where a departure is made from this the complex wording is employed to help young minds to usefully expand their lexicons. Some words and phrases are explained in brackets in the text, others by use of footnotes. There is a glossary of sorts included in the back of the book explaining the meaning, at least the meaning of the writers.

The authors have elsewhere written collections of essays concerning subjects of worldwide concern to them and other serious-minded people. Here an effort is made to mostly ignore those blood-curdling events seen daily in the news, and concentrate on some of the basic tenets of society which allow people and animals to live in harmony. These simple, easily grasped modern day animal fables teach basic truths, which can be foundation stones for readers to grow into responsible, hardworking members of our country's future.

The words found in the Bible at Micah 6:8 tell us our Creator only requires three simple things from us. Throughout the Three Cat Stories, these three requirements are recognized. The stars of the stories seek justice for others and themselves. They show mercy for others, especially for the less fortunate, and they show a measure of humility. This is not indicative of perfection or never falling short of best practice ..., after all they are just cats.

Hopefully, these collections of fanciful tales will enjoy a wide audience of both readers and hearers. This presumes a wide spectrum of English speaking people from different strati of society. It is the sincere hope of the authors that nothing in this book should ever be seen as in bad taste or derogatory to anyone.

Although the text indicates the geographical setting is in a mid-sized city in a coastal location, there is no intention to identify it with any specific locale. The three cats are the figments of an overstressed imagination. The persons named and identified, as well as stores, churches, organizations, etc. are all random and we feel sorry for anyone they resemble.

The writers are an elderly couple of great grandparents, who prayerfully hope the present dire circumstances in the world may improve during our present very young ones' lifetimes. We see our great nation writhing in what appears to us to be what Judge Robert Bork described a decade ago as *Slouching Towards Gomorrah.* The difference being, we no longer slouch, but are tumbling head over heels.

If the holders of our horrendous national debt should say "Never mind, what's a few trillion dollars between enemies?," if the Jihadists should all turn from their evil madness, and if God's people should humble themselves, and pray and seek His face and turn from their wicked ways, things would be better. All things considered, probably these things will be preempted by Jesus Christs' triumphant return for His children.

Meanwhile, we hope you can enjoy reading these innocent moral fables to tykes and recalling them to yourself and sharing them with others. Promote their purchase among your friends, knowing each sale benefits the designated owner, The Gilbertex Foundation, Inc. Such royalties are used to support Christian missionaries and programs at home and abroad.

We hope every time you see a cat, or especially three cats together, you may have a smile remembering the Three Cats Tales contained here. In the world of cinema they say "That's a wrap" while here we say "That's the plug in the jug."

Shirley & Vernon Gilbert – August, 2015

Three Cats Tails-er-Tales Glossary

Listed here are a few words used that may need explaining what the authors meant to mean.

ASAP – As Soon As Possible.
Apparent – plain to see, unhidden, noticeable
Apprehensive – Worried – concerned.
Affable – likeable, friendly.
Aversion – dislike, wish to be rid of.
Bee in someone's bonnet – something that bothers someone.
Benefactors – receivers, gainers, those supported.
Biddy – slang expression for a female chicken hen, or other female.
Brash – pert, loud, brassy, impulsive.
Bunt – pushing or shoving as with a butting action.
Catered – aided – supported – assisted- provided on order.
Cowered – retreating, or standing in fear.
Cuffed – placed in handcuffs – restrained.
Circa – about, more or less, near the date of.
Cranky – irritable, peevish, hard to please.
Demurred – turned down – refused.
Duo – two persons – a pair.
EMT – emergency medical technician.
Emulating – acting like, mimicking, aping.
ER – emergency room at a hospital.
Espied – seen, noticed.
Eureka - "I have found it" (from Greek).
Frisked – searched a suspect for illegal stuff.
Foraging – looking for food or supplies.
Habitat – Area where something is usually found.
IED—Improvised Explosive Device used against U.S. and coalition forces in Iraq and elsewhere.
Kiosk – booth, stand.
Limo – short for limousine, a long, stretched luxury car.
Miscreant – evil doer, bad guy.
Origin – start, beginning, seed.
Panorama – scene – view.
Perp – perpetrator, one doing evil, suspect.
Perplexed – puzzled, wondering.

Plagiarism – stealing another's writing, illegally copying.
Pro-bono – free, no charge, services rendered for no fee. Lawyers' lingo.
Purloined – stolen, taken illegally.
Regimen – plan, diet, system.
Sojourn – short trip – side trip.
Sleep on – delay – put off while deciding.
Stereotype – custom, mental image
Terrain – place or land for a certain use or purpose.
Uey – slang for U-turn – reversing course.
Unison – as one, united, with common goals.
Throw in the towel – quit, give up, stop contending, cry uncle.
Timorous – timid, shy, unsure, undecided
Variance – change, departure from normal, variation.
Venue – location, site, place, area of note.
Vile – evil – bad – nasty – not nice.

List of Names, Locations and Characters

Alfred – Mrs. Pennyrich's driver, butler and handyman.
Martin family – nearby, with yap yap dog.
Centerville – town where three cats live.
Cherry & Elm Avenues – streets at end of cat's alley.
Havenwood Retirement Village – retirement/nursing home.
Main Street – nearby busy street running across Avenues.
Mrs. Olsen – near neighbor with a parakeet.
Mrs. Pennymore – near neighbor with nice quilt.
Mrs. Pennyrich – wealthy widow on Sterling Street with dog named Brutus.
Mrs. Hazalott– Mrs. Pennyrich's friend.
Otto's Meat Market – shop of nice Mr. Otto, friend of the three cats.
Sergeant O'Malley – policeman friend of three cats.
Three Cats Service Center – vehicle servicing place named after the three cats.

* * * * * * * * * * * *

Printed in the United States
By Bookmasters